In a While, crocodile

Rohan Mahajan is a dynamic force at the intersection of governance, intellect, and grassroots innovation. A lawyer by education and a national campaign strategist by profession, Rohan has collaborated with several of the country's prominent political leaders, helping shape powerful narratives and election-winning strategies.

His academic foundation includes a Master's in Sustainable Development and a PGDM in Governance—credentials that reflect his deep commitment to policy-driven change and impact. Rohan is the founder of Sthaapna, a unique conclave platform that convenes young scholars, historians, and public thinkers to engage with India's civilizational knowledge and its relevance to contemporary governance and society. He also co-founded Swadhyay, a thoughtful series of magazines exploring the Indian education system, cultural history, and religious philosophy—each edition serving as a tribute to India's timeless intellectual traditions.

A former General Secretary and winner at the National Youth Parliament Organisation, Rohan is a powerful advocate for youth-led dialogue in democracy. He consistently brings fresh perspective, clarity, and strategic insight to every platform he engages with. In addition to his policy and public engagement work, Rohan is also the founder of Anushthan Idea Labs, a growing digital marketing agency that combines creative storytelling with data-driven strategies to support businesses, institutions, and political campaigns in building meaningful digital identities.

What makes Rohan's vision truly holistic is his integration of physical discipline with intellectual rigor. A state-level swimmer, avid marathon runner, and daily practitioner of yoga and pranayam, he channels the philosophy of balance, focus, and endurance into every aspect of his life and leadership.

Blending governance, grassroots activism, and creative entrepreneurship, Rohan Mahajan represents a new generation of Indian thinkers—grounded in tradition, driven by purpose, and equipped to inspire change.

In a While, crocodile

ROHAN MAHAJAN

Om Books International

First published in 2026 by

Om Books International

Corporate & Editorial Office
A-12, Sector 64, Noida 201 301
Uttar Pradesh, India
Phone: +91 120 477 4100
Email: editorial@ombooks.com
Website: www.ombooksinternational.com

Sales Office
107, Ansari Road, Darya Ganj,
New Delhi 110 002, India
Phone: +91 11 4000 9000
Fax: +91 11 2327 8091
Email: sales@ombooks.com
Website: www.ombooks.com

ISBN: 978-93-6395-728-2

Printed in India

10 9 8 7 6 5 4 3 2 1

To her,
You once said, 'Ro! I want a love story.'
Hence, I am writing one for you.

Contents

Prologue

Meeting Sonakshi

EVERY second made Rudra feel like he was a tong ready to go under a hammer. Sitting on a chair beside a table he had reserved for a date, he absent-mindedly listened to the girl in front of him. Sonakshi Arora kept yapping about her many accolades for what seemed like eternity. If he had known how she was beforehand, he wouldn't have agreed to this date. He could blame the algorithm for this, but how can the latter judge her character? He had taken a chance, and this chance had led him to this insane futility.

Psychology… psychiatry… narcissism… there were many scientific terms for people like her. But it didn't matter if he could even remember what the exact term was. She appeared to be selfish, manipulative, and cunningly charming, and definitely didn't want someone like her to be his life partner.

Being in the field of politics, he had become an excellent judge of a person's character. He could tell that this girl was as self-absorbed as anyone could be. Her attitude was a great put-off, but it was something he had expected. All his dates until now had been a tremendous disappointment. This one was simply larger.

As she talked away, the upscale restaurant felt like a gilded cage. He regretted picking the place. It was a rookie mistake made by a desire to impress, something he now cursed. Why had he been so shallow and superficial? He knew he would end up paying for the date, something that wouldn't have bothered him if the date had been worth remembering.

He kept staring at how animatedly and incessantly she talked. She moved her hands while she spoke, and though these gestures were supposed to draw him in, they turned him away. The entire talk of hers seemed rehearsed, as though she had prepared herself before the date, as anyone would for a play or a script rendition. She seemed more interested in showing off her personality than in a genuine connection. And he was beginning to feel tired of it. He felt his mind drift away, trying to move somewhere far away from her rambling. He watched her animated face and knew for sure that it was a lost cause.

His mind elsewhere, his fingers traced the rim of the glass in front of him. Its surface felt cold to him.

Cold, maybe because deep inside, he felt the heat of his frustration.

He just wanted to leave. He wished the waiter would magically appear with their bill.

A sigh escaped his mouth. How could he find the person he was meant to be with if people on dating apps were all like Sonakshi?

"And then I told my manager," Sonakshi continued, her tone rising dramatically, her eyes wide as if she had said something incredibly profound.

This isn't it. I don't want to be with someone like her.

He pulled his fingers away from the glass. Enough was enough. He'd spent what felt like a lifetime here, each boring minute an agonising torture.

"I'm sorry," he cut through her monologue. "Just remembered an important work commitment, so I need to leave right now."

The moment he uttered those words, he knew it was a lousy and cliched excuse.

As expected, Sonakshi stopped, a frown deepening the creases on her forehead.

"Oh… okay!" she replied in a flat but surprised voice.

Guilt hit him hard. A fleeting wish that he could have ended things more gracefully passed through his mind. But what else could he do? His frustration had eaten up all his patience.

He settled the bill and left a more generous tip than he intended. He felt it was the least he could do to make up for being rude.

The moment he stepped out of the restaurant, a cool breeze kissed his face. It felt so liberating, as though he had just been released from a prison where he had served a long, undeserved sentence. Mumbai winters were arriving, though he knew he could do without warm thermals.

He stretched his arms, his shoulders relaxing.

There was no sound around him except for the engine roar of a Bullet zipping its way past the parking lot towards the gate that led on to the road beyond.

"Rudra! Hey!"

He turned to his right, his eyes landing on two of his acquaintances from the political party headquarters where he volunteered. Ashok Chauhan and Harish Shetty. He couldn't really call them close friends or anything, but at the moment, anyone was better than the self-absorbed character he had just left behind.

"Oh, hello, Ashokbhai, Harishbhai!" he greeted. "What're you both doing here?"

He had not expected them at such an upscale restaurant. Or anywhere around it, for that matter.

"There's a pub across this parking lot," Rudra replied, grinning. "Join us?"

"What's the occasion?" he asked, surprised and excited at the invitation. "Any good news?"

He wondered if the political party had announced some good news.

"No.. no… nothing like that… there's this stand-up comedy show happening there," Harish said excitedly.

"Oh… then absolutely!" Rudra responded, the prospect of a stand-up comedy show seeming infinitely better than a date with Sonakshi.

"Come on… let's go!" he said. He took a step forward, ready to leave, when he heard a familiar voice.

"Oh, so this is the work you had to do!" Sonakshi shouted from behind, her voice cutting through his ears. Hurt and accusation twisted her face. "You can't just walk away after wasting my time. If you weren't interested, you could've had the decency to be honest about it."

He stood stunned.

Wasted her time? Really? All through the date, it had felt like his time was being wasted.

And why was she angry? Had she not really understood the cliched excuse? Did she actually believe him when he had said…?

It was common knowledge that a dating partner would excuse himself or herself from the date halfway if they felt it was not going anywhere. Work was usually the common excuse, the other one being family emergencies. Sometimes, a close friend would call them in response to a help signal.

But she had disregarded all of this. Had she been invested in him? Had she felt something for him?

His friends simply stared at both of them, surprised and amused.

He had seen his walk-away as a simple rejection. Sonakshi had felt something else. Insult perhaps. Or even something deeper.

He didn't know what to do. Should he offer an explanation? Should he apologise? Of course, it would be the right thing to do. He could have ended things gracefully, but he had been a little rude in his tone. Her eyes were flaring with hurt, and she fidgeted where she stood, her hands crossed against her bosomy chest.

No word came out of him in answer, though his throat caught in a discomforting knot.

She scowled at him, turned abruptly when he would not speak, and walked away.

"I really did not like you," he muttered behind her back, the words barely audible. He knew she couldn't hear him, but he wanted to believe that he had somehow said the words he had been feeling this whole time.

A part of him wished he could turn back time and find a better way to end the date.

A stronger part of him knew he wasn't wrong. Sonakshi wasn't his match, no matter what the dating app had said.

Chapter 1

It's a Match

KAVYA Kapoor worked in her little studio in an upscale area of Thane, right on the side of a busy Pokhran Road. She had only purchased this place a few months ago after paying a heavy deposit. Loans and easy monthly instalments made up the rest of the payments. Looking at the studio now, she felt excited about it. She had taken the first step to achieving her dream of being a fashion entrepreneur.

The studio had little square windows on either side of the door. It was not just the sunlight that they let stream in, but also the constant humdrum of vehicles honking. At first, the honking angered her, but she couldn't solve the problem. Vehicles lined up in a haphazard manner in front of her studio during the peak hours, waiting for the signal a couple of hundred meters away to turn green.

Even today, it was the incessant noise that took her away from her happy trance. Grunting, she stood and walked among the circular trolleys upon which hangers perched. Very few of them were empty. Many had clothes and apparel hung on them, all having vibrant patterns of her designs. There was not one design she was not proud of. Also, the fact that she sourced the cloth through rurally placed artisans made her even prouder.

When she had told her father her plan a year or two ago, he had invested in her venture and provided her with the seed money, despite being a traditionalist who looked askance at entrepreneurship. She had used this to pay the studio's rather hefty deposit.

Even though her business had been doing well of late, her life had begun to feel empty. Most of her friends chalked it down to loneliness. Many of them, who were now happily married, took the initiative to hook her up with the other singles they knew, but so far, none of her dates had succeeded. And that's when her friends chided her for being so picky and choosy. Her best friend, Sonakshi, had insisted that she try out this new dating app called App-atched. Sonakshi had told her how she had many eventful dates through it.

Kavya was aware of what 'eventful' meant in Sonakshi's context. Oftentimes, it meant a one-night stand.

She, however, did not wish for that kind of relationship. She recognised the need for physical intimacy, but she wouldn't copy her best friend and seek it in the name of a successful date. What she craved was an emotional affair, something Sonakshi and the rest of her friends may have felt happy about. After all, they had, in most probability, thought that she would give up on dating and relationships after a really bad one in the recent past. The heartbreak from it had lasted one entire month, even though the decision to break up had been hers.

Dating apps, though, did nothing to entice her. To her, they were more for people who sought hookups and situationships rather than a true romantic commitment.

"Try kar na yaar!" Sonakshi had insisted. "Who knows… you might just find someone who appreciates your art and your passion."

She had downloaded the app some time ago, but she had not opened it.

Until now.

She took a deep breath, her fingers hovering over the app icon on her Android phone. It felt silly, almost frivolous, amidst her demanding schedule and her serious and ambitious goals. Still, perhaps this was worth a try. Sonakshi had told her that this app was different… that this app had good people. Sant Mahatmas, she called them. Kavya couldn't be more annoyed about it.

Tapping the icon open, she began to swipe through the profiles. Most of the pictures were staged, and the bios were quite generic, like those generated by AI chatbots. After swiping a few, she wished Sonakshi were here so she could accuse her of wasting her time with this app. There was no profile on this that she could relate to. And, just when she was about to close it, her eyes caught the profile of a dashing fellow, but one that was unaware he was being candidly clicked.

The young man in the photo wasn't posing or flexing. Instead, the photographer had just captured him mid-laugh, his eyes crinkling at the corners, his face lit up with a genuine warmth. Compared to the images and profiles she had been seeing, this profile seemed authentic. His bio was simple: Passionate about making a difference in my community. And maybe some good chai.

He didn't seem to be someone from corporate life who was looking for a companion who could push up his status. From all the photos he had uploaded, he was preaching what he practised. And that captured her attention.

"Hmmm… interesting!" she murmured to herself, a small smile playing on her lips. She scrolled through his profile, the rest of the photos revealing bits and pieces of his life. There was a shot of him at a community rally, another one of him laughing with a group of homeless kids on the street, and yet another of him with a bunch of people who seemed like his colleagues at some big corporate office.

"What do you think, Leela?" she asked her assistant, who just flitted past her. "Is this guy a winning cause or a losing one?"

Leela peered into her phone. "Well, bio and photos seem encouraging, but people often lie in such places like these… I don't know how this particular app vets the profiles and their characters, but maybe… maybe you can give this fellow a try. His profile seems genuine. Maybe this is a good way to get back into the dating scene?"

"He seems different," she chuckled, "I think I might actually like him, but then again, as you said, it seems too good to be true. Might end up disappointing me, no?"

"Well, you'll never know unless you try," Leela said. "Give him a try."

Kavya took another deep breath and tapped the heart icon on the man's profile.

Anticipation grew in her heart, and even as she waited to see whether he would respond, she resumed her work and went through her books of accounts.

Rudra Rathore had chosen a distinct career for himself. The members of his small community back in Nashik did not agree with his choice and often judged him for it. According to them, someone from the working middle-class section of society had no business choosing politics as a career. You could be an engineer, a doctor, a lawyer, but never a politician. "Leave all these matters to the rich or the union leaders of the poor," one of the elderly men would say to him whenever he visited his parents' place.

Though everyone considered his choice irregular and weird, it did not stop him from entering the arena. He worked through the ranks and cadres of a nationalistic political party diligently, but he did not let that be his only definition. He also worked as the Vice-President of

Governance Affairs for a multi-national company, where he worked for their best interests and represented them to the government authorities. Most evenings, he volunteered his time at the party's campaign office, working on their various schemes and projects.

The current work at the party office involved the Independence Day event and the 'Ghar Ghar Tiranga' campaign that preceded it. The party office also had to address election campaigning, but gave it lower priority, postponing it until after Independence Day. Given the results of the latest elections, the party headquarters had sent a missive to all of its workers to improve the party's image among the people, yes. To do so, the ruling government, amidst much opposition, had announced and implemented many schemes, including one that benefited the female population of the state.

Rudra sat in his cluttered office, breathing the scent of stale chai and listening to the faint hum of a perpetually overworked ceiling fan. Piles of pamphlets, campaign posters, and half-eaten packets of chips sat on his desk, different to the one at his corporate office. Back there, it was as though he had little to no work. Here, it was as though he had plenty of work pending.

The clock on the wall ticked relentlessly, reminding him of the endless to-do list. A sigh escaped his mouth as he ran a hand through his already tousled hair. Today had been a brutal day of endless meetings and frustrated negotiations with political leaders and influential volunteers. After a particularly gruelling time, he decided he needed a break. At that moment, anything was better than drafting government policies or organising rallies.

Recently, his friends had been pestering him to try out a new dating app, claiming it was the 'modern solution' to his loneliness problem. From his latest experience of that horrible date with Sonakshi, he didn't expect a lot from the app. Neither did he believe that he would find his life partner on it. He had tried a lot of apps, but their algorithms failed in their task to match him up with someone compatible with him. He felt that this app would, like others, do no better.

He had reluctantly downloaded it and created a profile on it. He had uploaded select photos depicting his community work and kept his bio as simple as possible compared to the other profiles, which he found mostly to be show-offs.

After the busy day that was today, he needed a distraction. If this app could provide it, he would take it.

Scrolling through, he found most profiles not so memorable, just as he expected. Frustrated, he was ready to delete it altogether when a notification buzzed on his phone, and his thumb froze.

Some girl had 'hearted' his profile.

He clicked on the bell-shaped notifications icon in the top right-hand corner. A tab opened up. The notification read, Kavya Kapoor liked your profile. You have a match!

Curious, he clicked on the notification.

The girl's profile flashed on his screen.

The girl was a gorgeous young woman with kind eyes and a radiant smile. Her profile pic showed her laughing, and her bio, like his, was simple, describing her work with the local artisans and her love of traditional arts and crafts.

A woman after my heart.

"Aha!" he muttered, a small smile tugging at the corner of his lips.

He scrolled through her profile and looked at the photos she had uploaded. Most of the images in her profile showcased her beautiful designs, and when there was indeed a photo of her person in them, it was no generic selfie. Most of her photos were of her at her workplace.

He went over her bio again. And what he read there made him feel as if she might be the one.

Working with the rural artisans and providing a platform for them to connect with the gracious consumers.

There was more.

Quite a lengthy one compared to his.

But he did not go to read it further. He simply tapped on the heart icon, hoping against hope that this girl was not like Sonakshi.

He turned to his assistant, who was organising some files. "Hey, Neha," he said, "ever tried one of these dating apps?"

Neha giggled. "You? Mr Campaign-Organiser-Extraordinaire?" she asked. "I didn't take you for a romantic."

Rudra chuckled. "Well, even I deserve a bit of a distraction, right? This one… she seems… different." He gestured vaguely to his phone. "She's into local arts and crafts. Very unlike the people I meet every day."

"Well, good luck, boss," Neha answered with a knowing smile. "Hope you finally find someone who has the patience to tolerate your political rants."

He nodded and kept his phone down. But every moment after, Kavya liked you; you've a match rang in his ears. He paused midway, his hands holding a venue permit document signed by the local authorities.

Surprise had taken him when he learned that the girl had indeed up-swiped him. Taking his phone again, he scrolled once more through her photos. And when he was done, he longed to send her a message. His fingers hovered over the tiny button, shaped like a brown envelope, unsure of his approach.

Flirting was beyond his skill level. All those lovey-dovey sweet lines that boys spoke to impress girls were a challenge to him. Yet, Kavya's profile made him want to try. She was different, interesting, and he felt a pull to get to know her better.

He bit his lip, his mind already trying to figure out the best way to start a conversation. He didn't want to appear too eager, but he also wanted to start a conversation that would pique her interest. After much deliberation, he decided to go with a straightforward approach. He typed a message, deleted it, typed another one, deleted that one as well, and then finally settled on something that felt natural.

RR: Hey Kavya, your profile is very interesting. Love your work with the artisans. It's very important work.

Pausing, he stared at the screen, questioning his decisions. He wanted to give her an opening to talk about her passion for the arts without making him seem shallow or too eager. He debated whether to include a witty line or two or a more quirky sentence. But then he decided against it.

He sent the message and then closed the app, reminding himself he still had a meeting to plan. As he resumed his work, he found himself distracted. His mind kept flitting to Kavya. He felt a pull towards her he could not easily ignore. A sense that she was someone special. Someone he would want to connect with on a deeper level.

He was about to dive into the logistics of the community gathering when his phone buzzed again.

It was a notification from the app.

KK: Hi, Rudra, thanks for the message. It's nice to see that someone cares for the traditional arts and crafts. What are you passionate about?

A smile broke across his face.

RR: Well, aside from trying to fix our local government, I'm passionate about… making a good cup of chai. Maybe we could discuss our passions over a cuppa?

After pressing 'Send', excitement bubbled inside him. He had taken a chance, a step forward. If she replied with a yes, his elation would know no bounds.

He leaned back against his chair, letting out a small sigh. He wanted to know where all this could lead.

Chapter 2

And We Met

RUDRA had agreed to Kavya's suggestion that they meet in Nashik as both of them were in the same city for a few days. They had arrived at the time and location after a long discussion on the dating app's messaging system.

When his watch flashed 4:15, a curse escaped his mouth as he feared being late on his first date.

A ping on his phone alerted him to Kavya's recent message.

KK: Hello?

He moved to reply just then, but Rohit from the party head office called to discuss important matters. The call resulted in some boisterous discussions and would have continued had it not been for a tut-tut sound interrupting it.

Seeing the blinking screen, he saw an incoming call from Kavya.

Apologising profusely, he disconnected the call with Rohit and switched to Kavya's.

"You reached?" he asked, keeping his voice steady.

"I'm already there… been sitting here for a while.."

The hint of disappointment in her voice made him wince.

He froze for a moment, wondering if he had stereotyped her with the usual fashionably late crowd. Obviously, Kavya wasn't like them. Just as he had thought when he had responded to her upswipe, she felt different.

Her penchant for time was perhaps the result of her work as a project manager at a multinational corporation. Her LinkedIn profile sported meticulously detailed passages, each skill endorsed by many of her connections. Every testimonial praises her punctuality.

His hands trembled slightly as he turned off the ignition. He got out of the car and raced to the building that housed the cafe.

A long queue at the elevator and the elevator's floor position blinking on the crimson dial made him opt for the stairs. In his hurry, he sometimes ended up taking two of them at a time. By the time he reached the third floor, his shirt, carefully ironed that morning, began to cling to his back.

The warm glow of Sand Oak Cafe spilt out to meet him. Through the open doors, the rich aroma of roasted coffee beans wafted into his nose, making the cafe even more inviting than its plush ambience. Gasping for breath, he waited for a second or two.

Somewhere in the distance, the second hand of the clock ticked forward, making him realise he was already late. Straightening up, he entered the cafe and looked about. He found her sitting at a table by the window, a curtain framing her silhouette in the soft, late afternoon light. The way she sat on the chair was commanding enough, her posture straight and stern.

If someone asked him to write an essay to describe her style, he would write it as corporate elegance. The black trousers and a crisp black-and-white checked shirt told him she valued corporate etiquette more. The small silver hoops in her ears caught the light as she turned her head to see him approach.

His eyes marvelled at her hair gathered into a sleek bun, secured with a silver stick. The bunstick looked more like an elegant sculpture than a mere hair accessory. Everything about her screamed attention to detail.

This was everything he was not. He was more of a last-minute planning and casual disregard for time kind of guy.

His throat suddenly dry, he approached the table. Their hands met in a brief, formal shake. Her soft skin felt warm to him despite her firm grip.

"Hello," he managed a greeting, hoping to mask his embarrassment for coming late.

"You should never keep a lady waiting, you know," she said, arching her eyebrows playfully. Heat rose in his face.

Her dark eyes held his, and he found himself struggling to look away.

"Oh… I was just downstairs in my car…," he began and then stopped himself. Excuses wouldn't work on someone like her. "I should've realised you'd reach early. I'm really sorry, and I promise it won't happen again." The sincerity in his voice surprised even him.

A small smile played at the corner of her lips. "Well, at least you're honest about it. Most men would have made up some elaborate excuse about traffic."

He could not deny the energy about her. An energy that pulled him closer to her.

She had this confidence in her that made his self-assured demeanour falter. For the first time in his life, he felt control slipping away from him. To his surprise, a small part of him liked it.

As soon as he sat down, the waiter approached them with the menus.

They browsed through their menus, although that did not stop him from stealing glances at her.

A strange energy vibrated inside him. Her features enticed him, especially the tiny mole on the side of her nose. Her smile made his heart race and his anxiety disappear.

"So," she said, closing the menu and keeping it aside, "tell me something that's not on your dating profile."

On most of the dates he had gone on, he initiated the conversation. Today, though, she had taken it upon herself to start. He promised himself not to underestimate this woman again.

"You first," he said.

She laughed and then started to talk about her family and friends, her hobbies and passions, and how she had gotten into her entrepreneurial venture. She spoke so fast that sometimes he found it difficult to keep up.

"Hey, ermmm… I'm actually a slow listener," he admitted. "And I take time to process my thoughts, so try to be a bit slow, and I'll try to be a bit fast."

She snickered, raising her hands in mock surrender, an unexpected gesture coming from a composed person like her.

"So, what else are you interested in other than politics?" she asked, directing her beautiful, penetrating eyes at him again.

"I'm a fine astrologer," he replied, feeling more at ease as they moved into familiar territory.

"Oh, really?" she asked, her eyebrows shooting up.

He nodded. "Let me show you a sample…. What year were you born? What time?"

"4 in the morning." A mischievous smile played on her lips. "When I was born, maybe the music around me would be like 'chaar baj gaye lekin party abhi baaki hain'."

He checked her horoscope mentally, calculating her ascendant, her moon sign. He smiled, recognising how it fit her perfectly. Her personality was indeed like the moon. Calm, humorous, yet dominating like a mother. When he shared this, she clapped her hands in delight, the action drawing several stares from the nearby tables.

"Mine is sun, by the way," he added softly. "Perhaps we're here for a reason."

She sneezed right then, breaking the moment.

"Are you okay?" he asked, concerned.

"Na… just a little cold."

He understood. He had just recovered from a cold a week ago. The sneezing and the coughing could be irritating.

"If you're not well, we could have this meet some other day," he said, guilt twisting his stomach inside.

"No, no, I'm fine… It's just the after-effects from walking in the rain last night."

Guilt tightened inside him again as he remembered the conversation he had had the previous night.

RR: What're you up to?

KK: Thinking of going out for a walk, but it's raining outside.

RR: It's just a drizzle… don't think you'll get so wet… besides, these are just pre-monsoon showers.

KK: Hmmm… I don't mind being wet…. just that I've a few important things to do at the studio… I don't want to be sick.

RR: Loosen up… these rains won't make you sick… but just in case, carry an umbrella… Nashik rains are unpredictable.

KK: Right… will talk to you later then… decided that I will go outside, drizzle or not.

He should not have encouraged her to go out in the rain. She might not have gotten the cold otherwise.

Wanting to make amends, he suggested, "Let's order something? What're you having?"

He passed her the menu, watching as she studied it with the same focus as she probably gave her project reports.

When the waiter arrived, Rudra ordered first. "Beer for me… 500 ml large… freshly brewed."

"Gin with tonic water," Kavya said decisively.

"No tonic water available," the waiter informed them.

Kavya sighed, fidgeting on the chair. "Gin with water and lime juice then."

The waiter noted their orders down on his pad. "Anything to eat, Ma'am, Sir?"

She looked at him questioningly. A familiar flutter in his stomach made him squirm a little under her gaze.

He wasn't particularly hungry, but he could tell that she was. Hunger reflected in her eyes. "I'm really bad at choosing food… so you order for me too."

"Please… choose something," she insisted.

"Hmmm… okay, one veg galouti kebab."

"A risotto, please," she ordered. "You can trust risottos anywhere. I always order that whenever I am not sure or I'm not sure of the food in the place. It's always a safe bet."

The waiter arrived with their drinks promptly.

He watched her as she mixed her 60ml of gin with water and lime juice. Once she had finished preparing her drink, she looked up at him. "So, Rudra, what's there?"

He frowned, realising he had been looking diagonally to her right, his gaze wandering as it had done so most evenings.

"I'm used to undivided attention, you should know," she said. There was a hint of authority there that made his pulse quicken.

Rudra had always been shy on his first date with someone. It did not matter that he had been on so many of them. That same shyness plagued him right now.

"Sorry," he apologised and forced himself to make eye contact with her.

She acknowledged him with a nod, apparently satisfied.

"Well, now, can you tell me about your past relationships?" he asked, surprising himself with his boldness.

She laughed, a soft sound that seemed to warm the space between them. "Well, three, if you must know. And then there was this boy I liked when I was in school. He liked me too, but he went abroad. We write emails to each other now… and he's become a pastor… or he might be gay for all I know… so don't count this as one." She took a sip of her drink before continuing. "And the three that I spoke about… one was Taran. I was young and crazy for him. He proposed marriage, and I said yes. But then I came to realise that he wasn't right for me. I had introduced him to Dad and all, and he said the boy really didn't have any spine. By then, I had begun to see that our relationship was toxic and, hence, ended things. The other two were relatively paltry affairs. One was with a whiny guy named Manav. The other one was Dhruv."

Her openness surprised him. Rudra rarely kept track of anyone's past, but something about her made him want to know everything.

After finishing her drink, they moved to the lobby for a smoke. He felt a pang of disappointment when he couldn't offer her preferred brand, and she seemed genuinely sad about it. He offered to share one of his, but she declined firmly, showing that streak of independence he was coming to admire.

When they returned to their table, his eyes betrayed him again, drifting to that spot diagonally from her.

"Rudra, what's there again?"

"Oops, sorry again," he straightened, forcing himself to focus.

Their food arrived. She ate with obvious hunger. He found himself watching her, fascinated by her elegance even while obviously famished.

"Hot water, please!" she called out to a passing waiter, her tone carrying that natural authority he had noticed earlier. "Got a cold, so don't want to risk drinking much," she said, turning to me.

The conversation turned to work, and he found himself opening up about his political career. "I am a volunteer at a political party… currently working with a senior politician. I take care of the national campaigns and the organisational work." He explained how politics was a different profession and the challenges of sustaining oneself in such a turbulent environment. "I was recently appointed as the vice president of government affairs at one company." He had achieved more than he was telling her, but he didn't want to share everything at once. Perhaps because it was too early. Mostly because her interest appeared to be waning.

"And what about you?" he asked, eager to shift the focus back to her. As she began to speak about her corporate life, Rudra found himself fully engaged, his wandering gaze finally settling on her face, captured by the way her eyes lit up as she described her work. Maybe it was the gin or the lingering effects of his cold, but he felt something shift inside him. This didn't feel like a first date at all. It felt as though he had known her forever.

The sun and moon had indeed aligned tonight. For once, he didn't mind being outshone.

"Actually," Kavya said, her eyes lighting up with a different kind of enthusiasm, "I started with something small in Bhandup." Her fingers moved deftly across her phone screen, pulling up images of ethnic designs that made Rudra lean in closer.

"You'll be famous for these one day," he mumbled, watching how she beamed at the compliment. There was something magnetic about her pride in her work, the way her entire demeanour changed when discussing her passion projects.

They stepped out for another smoke break, and once again, Rudra found himself wanting to offer her one of his cigarettes.

"Are you sure you won't share mine?" he asked, holding out his pack.

"No," she said firmly, but with a smile that softened the rejection. Her independence was becoming increasingly endearing to him.

Back at their table, his eyes betrayed him again, drifting to that familiar spot diagonal to her.

"Rudra," she said, her tone carrying that now-familiar mix of authority and affection. "Eyes here, please."

He straightened up, embarrassed but charmed by her directness. Somehow, he found himself talking about politics again, watching her interest slowly fade despite her polite nods.

The clock ticked to 6:45. "I'll leave around 7, I think," she said.

Panic fluttered in Rudra's chest. He was losing her to his political monologues.

"So, tell me," he said quickly, changing tack, "what's your experience been like? Meeting guys for marriage experience?" He held his breath, hoping she wouldn't find the question too forward.

Her expression shifted, becoming more animated. "Recently, I met this guy named Ritvik who has this spiritual startup…" She paused, considering her words. "I've met him thrice, but then I realised he wasn't clear…I mean, he hadn't gotten over his past relationships. So, I stepped back."

Rudra nodded, mentally noting how she valued emotional clarity. This woman demanded complete attention, unwavering clarity, and absolute exclusivity. Qualities he found himself wanting to provide.

"I have no rush to get married," she added, her eyes drifting to the clock again. It read 7:10.

"Will leave in ten minutes," she announced.

"Okay," Rudra said, gathering his courage. "Will you mind meeting tomorrow, as I am in Nashik and mostly free?"

She raised an eyebrow, amusement dancing in her eyes. "Rush karna hain?" The Hinglish slipped out naturally, making her seem more approachable.

"No… not at all…" he fumbled, suddenly feeling like a teenager asking for a second date. "I was just… erm… mostly free, and I thought we could meet up for maybe a coffee or something."

She considered this, her project manager's mind probably analysing all angles, before her face softened. "Yes, we can definitely do that…"

His heart soared at her response.

As they left the café at seven-thirty, he found himself noticing her bunstick again. "Nice bunstick!" he commented, pleased when her face lit up.

"Oh, thanks," she said, touching it briefly. "I've got two of these already, and a porcupine one too… What I don't have is a golden bunstick."

The information lodged itself in his mind like a precious secret. It sounded like a future gift idea, if ever they reached that stage.

The thought made him smile. Such a smile as he had not had for a long time.

Chapter 3

Second Date

As Rudra entered his home through the main door, he found the living room empty. It was weird since usually at this hour of the night, the house roared with noise. His father would be sitting on the couch watching TV while his mother would keep shouting at him to keep the volume down. The Rathore House in Nashik was no less noisy than the busiest street in Nashik.

"Mummy! Daddy!" he called out, but there was no response.

This felt even stranger. His parents usually never left their house this late at night, except that they had a function to attend. And this was rare, as most of his extended family lived in Rajasthan. They themselves had their origins in the northbound state, but had shifted to Nashik decades ago and built a life there. He had been born and brought up here, only moving to Mumbai for his career later.

Where had his parents disappeared to?

He checked their bedroom to see if they had slept early, but the bed was empty. Sighing, he kept looking and checked out the kitchen last. On the refrigerator, he found a pinned note. Letters written in beautiful handwriting with a blue ink pen graced its paper. His mother's handwriting was unmistakable. His father could not write so beautifully. His parents had apparently decided to break the monotony of home-cooked food and went out to a nearby restaurant for dinner.

A smile made his lips curl.

Years had passed since they took time out for themselves. Why then, suddenly, had they decided to rekindle the romance between them out of the blue?

And for it to happen on the same day as he met Kavya, he couldn't feel happier.

Maybe it was kismet.

He wanted to call Kavya and tell her what happened, but he refrained from doing so, not wanting to disturb her, knowing full well she could be driving. He messaged instead.

RR: Home? Happy to see you. Looking forward to meeting you again.

KK: Likewise. And, no, I have not yet reached home. Too much traffic on the highway.

RR: Ping me once you reach home.

For some time, he paced about and kept looking at his phone. Why had she not replied yet? Did she not reach home?

His anticipation only grew in the meantime and then turned into impatience. His fingers moved to the dialer, wondering if he should call her and ask. But every time he went to press the dial icon, he retreated, not wishing to seem desperate.

Half an hour passed before his phone pinged again.

KK: Rudra, just reached home… I am sleepy now.

Rudra breathed deep.

RR: Get on a call?

KK: Hey, I sleep at 10:30… It's a habit of mine… maybe talk in the morning?

How different she was compared to him?

Kavya had a structured and disciplined routine. He was more spontaneous and impulsive.

With the prospect of a call denied, he jumped on his bed and slept, drifting off into dreams.

With the onset of dawn, his sleep broke. Rudra faced the warm morning light, irritated, and wished he could sleep more. After all, with his waking, his dream of Kavya had shattered and faded.

Reaching for his phone, he checked if there were any messages in the night. There was none.

He yearned to get in touch with her. She had refused the call at night. Morning, though, was a different time.

RR: Good morning. What are you up to?

KK: Surya Namaskars done. Now I'm listening to music and chilling.

RR: Surya Namaskars?

KK: Yes, I do them every day… twenty-one SNs after drinking 1.5 litres of water.

His eyes baulked at the message.

She's not only disciplined, but she's committed to health and wellness, too. My kind of girl.

Another ping on his phone took his mind off his thoughts.

KK: What's up with you?

RR: Going for a run soon.

KK: Cool. Watched any movie recently? Any recommendations?

RR: Chalte Chalte comes to mind.

KK: Great, I will put that on my watch list. I love watching movies in fragments. I like to savour each scene. So, pardon me if I don't respond to you with an immediate review.

Kavya had told him how much she loved watching movies, so he was surprised when she told him she had not yet watched *Chalte Chalte*. Maybe she wasn't a SRK fan. Hopefully, she'd see it soon and discuss it with him.

For the next forty minutes, he went on a run and covered seven kilometres, his pace fueled by joy, each stride made effortless by her thoughts.

Throughout the day, Rudra became glued to the phone, busy talking with the company executives and the party high command. At the same time, he did take time off to analyse the goings-on in the T20 Cricket World Cup happening this month. India was on a winning streak, but he quelled his excitement about it. Last time, India had dashed its way to the ODI World Cup final unbeaten and lost to Australia in the end. He decided not to put his expectations on his country winning the trophy.

The work became so extenuating that he called Kavya to ask if they could postpone their second meeting to another date. It made him happy that she understood him. She also told him she had work to look after, even though she was far away from her studio in Thane.

The twilight hour soon arrived, and Rudra became free from his work. He took out his phone and started messaging.

RR: Home?

KK: Going for a walk… will call once I'm on the terrace.

True to her word, twenty minutes later, his phone lit up with her call. The hour they spent talking thus felt like mere minutes; their conversation focused on random, mundane topics.

"Free tomorrow?" he asked, his heartbeat quickening. "Maybe for a beer or a coffee?"

Kavya's voice, a melody he was quickly getting addicted to, carried a smile as she replied, "Yes, we'll meet, but on the opposite side of the town."

He frowned but didn't voice his doubts. She must have a reason for wanting to meet on the other side of the town. Maybe she wanted to get away from prying eyes. Considering they both lived just a few blocks away from each other, it did not seem like an unfair request.

"Ok," he responded.

"3:45 at The Ulysses?" she proposed.

"The MIDC one?"

"Yes."

"Fine… okay," he confirmed, already counting the hours until their last meeting.

"See you tomorrow then."

He disconnected the call and then climbed down the stairs as his mother announced dinner, shouting at the top of her voice.

The morning sun had barely risen over the horizon when Rudra handed his carefully chosen dark jeans and a crisp light blue shirt to the laundry shop a couple of ways away from his house. He then selected his dark brown brogues with meticulous care, each of them neatly polished.

After a quick but heavy breakfast, he got busy with a couple of calls from Jagadeesh, his partner in their spiritual tourism venture. It had been something he had been working on side-by-side, wanting to be a part of the startup revolution, embracing the country. His talks had gone on so long that he didn't realise he had missed lunch.

His mother came twice to call him for lunch, but he kept telling her he would have it later. But when his calls were done, the clock read 2 P.M. Even though he could have his lunch now, he decided to forego it and save his appetite for his meeting later. His sister had used her position as an officer to secure for them a table before its usual 5 P.M. opening time. He hoped the meeting would be perfect.

At precisely 2:45, Rudra sent a message announcing his departure. Her swift reply, confirming she was en route as well, made his heart skip a beat. On the way, he stopped to buy cigarettes, adding a few extra to his pack. But, despite all his planning, he arrived at the venue a few minutes late. He slipped into the chair opposite her, breathless from running, afraid that he had made a poor impression again, being unpunctual. "I'm sorry," he apologised, his gaze lingering on her, taking in her appearance with barely concealed admiration.

"Chalta hai… It's not more than five minutes," she replied, sounding amused.

He smiled. After everything he had done, he had failed to arrive on time. The punctual woman that she was, he feared she wouldn't take kindly to his being late. To his surprise, she showed no anger towards him. Was it because he was only five minutes late? What would have happened if he had been more than five minutes late?

A sleek black dress clung to her frame, its fabric pretty elegant. He had a ranking suspicion that the dress was of her own design. Sunglasses perched atop her head like a sophisticated crown, and her hair was swept into an immaculate bun that drew attention to the graceful curve of her neck. The sight of her made the words he had chosen with utmost care and rehearsed feel inadequate.

Noticing her slight discomfort with the air-conditioning, Rudra stood without hesitation to adjust the vents. The cool air is now caressing her instead of blowing directly at her. She appreciated his gesture with a sweet`smile.

Very soon, they engaged in a conversation about the events happening in Nashik as they placed an order. She wanted to have gin with water and lime juice, while he wanted a pitcher of Budweiser. She told him how she wanted to be a popular fashion designer with recognition in niche circles, while he wanted to increase his political influence among the masses. It felt so good to be honest with her. It was a rare and precious feeling he could only have with her. He hadn't had this feeling when he had gone on other dates.

He could not tell when, but their conversation soon drifted to the topic of past relationships. She confessed to always missing something, an unnamed "better" waiting for her somewhere in the future. Rudra understood it completely. He, too, had been waiting for that 'better' someone.

"What's your idea of romance?" he asked.

She paused, as though considering her words with care. "I like to spend time… be vulnerable… and should feel free around the person."

When he pressed for more, she cleverly deflected by asking, "Why don't you answer your own?"

"My idea of romance is hopeless… I'm a hopelessly romantic kind of person… I'd hardly care about the world if I were in love."

She giggled.

As their drinks arrived, they shared glimpses of their ideal homes. Hers was filled with nature, music, and simple pleasures like morning oats and a refrigerator stocked with mangoes and chocolates. Peace and comfort defined his along with tightly tucked bedsheets and aloo parathas swimming in butter. Their lifestyles were quite contrasting, and yet, he felt getting closer to her was the only logical thing to do.

Three beers and three gins later, having shared a pizza, a sizzling platter, and her favourite risotto, they reluctantly prepared to leave around 7:45 P.M. They shook hands with each other, something Rudra found awkward given the intimacy they shared during the meeting. According to him, a mere physical touch as a handshake, couldn't capture the depth of their emotional connection.

During his drive home, Rudra's thoughts kept returning to her, each memory confirming what his heart had already accepted. She was the one.

RR: Always happy seeing you.

KK: Likewise, it will take another 15 mins to reach home.

RR: Will be heading for Thane tomorrow. Have to work on the Independence Day Campaign. Hoping that you'll display our Tiranga at both your home and studio on Independence Day. Will remind you.

She had agreed.

It brought a smile to his face.

Chapter 4

The Turbulence

THE Indian victory in the recent T20 Cricket World Cup brought happiness to the doors of many of his countrymen. People found a reason to celebrate every other weekend. Rudra, too, did not fall behind. He partied with his friends after work. On days when Kavya came to the studio, he would go and meet her. These visits had become pretty often of late. She would spend half the week in her studio, but in the evenings, they would go pub-hopping.

Even when they could not meet, they kept in touch over the phone and through the messaging system on the app. He wanted to delete it, now that he needed no more visits to other profiles. But when Kavya said that she preferred using the app for messaging, he submitted to her choice. After weeks of using it, he had gotten used to the app's interface. It was easy to use and simple, and its emoticons were just so alluring.

Time passed by with Independence Day barely a fortnight away. The Ghar Ghar Tiranga campaign proceeded in full flow. He became busy with the campaign work. Mr Sharma, one of the right-hand men of a local political party leader, had tasked him with drafting the speech for the Independence Day event at the head office. The campaign took a toll on the workers as they had to wade through the pitter-patter of heavy Mumbai rains. The monsoon threatened to drown their progress, but the workers endured on. He felt for them and did all he could to make his peers in the party office comfortable.

It was not just the party that viewed this campaign as important. The people with a nationalistic fervour also wished for this campaign to succeed. They wanted to bring back the country's pride in the eyes of the masses. The workers around him went from house to house, educating them on the importance of the Tiranga and requesting them to put one up on the balconies of their houses on the 15th of August. So far, the reports had been positive. This made him feel better.

Kavya did not blame him for not paying her as much attention as he should have. She actively supported him during the campaign by forwarding and reposting his campaign messages on social media. She promised him to hoist the Tiranga at her home and studio when the day came. They still found time to meet on some weekends and found some really good eateries in Thane.

He enjoyed spending time with her. Her company was something he looked forward to after a day's worth of gruelling work.

As he focused on his work today, he received a call from Kavya. She told him she would be coming to Thane five days later for a few days, and then would later head to an exhibition in Bharuch, Gujarat. She also told him of an upcoming shoot somewhere in the heart of Mumbai. A couple of her team members had apparently found her a location in Bandra. He admired her ability to maintain such a packed schedule and her willingness to carve out precious moments between responsibilities to connect with him.

Their conversation deepened as she steered them towards spirituality, a realm they both held sacred. Her curiosity about his religious knowledge resonated deeply within him. Very few had ever inquired about the deeper meaning behind the scriptures he had studied.

"Rudra, tell me…," her voice grew soft with genuine curiosity, "… why did Shri Ram leave Maata Sita in exile? And why did Shri Krishna leave Devi Radha?"

"I'll give you those answers, but in person," he promised. Some truths, he believed, deserved to be shared face-to-face rather than over a phone line.

She accepted his promise but then had to disconnect the call as work beckoned. Three days passed by without a talk on the phone, though they did keep in touch with each other over the app's messaging system. Two nights before she visited Thane, their talk ventured into challenging territory.

The LGBTQ community.

Kavya's question about his views forced him to confront the complex intersection of his personal beliefs and his public political persona.

"As a person, I'm accepting," he explained, trying to be as diplomatic as possible, "but as a politician, I've to consider societal perspectives. In our country, especially among the lower strata, it remains taboo. When I'm asked to take a stand publicly, I've to align with the majority view."

When her response came, he could hear a tinge of disappointment in her voice. "Rudra, if that's how you think, maybe we shouldn't be talking so much. I have a huge professional network where people are practising their choices. And I have a lot of friends from that community."

"It's okay," he said, not wishing for the topic to cause a broader chasm between them. "I don't have any issues with your connections. We both know there are laws now favouring this segment of people. I'm not against you thinking of their rights, but I've my limitations." He was caught between his personal conviction and his political pragmatism. His words, though, sounded hollow to him.

An abrupt end to their call made him wonder if he should simply have agreed with her perspective and not bare his own feelings with her. Though work beckoned him, he couldn't help but ponder over the delicate dance he was embroiled in. The conversations he had with her pushed him to examine beliefs he'd long taken for granted. Somehow, that didn't feel like a bad thing.

At least, he was telling himself it didn't.

The day finally arrived when Kavya had told him she would come. Early morning, he had received a message, which made him feel happy. For a time, he had thought she wouldn't, given how their last conversation had ended.

Rudra kept in touch with her as she travelled. The messages came swiftly whenever her network didn't go down. As soon as she got down at the Thane railway station, she gave him a call.

"What are your plans, bro?" he asked.

"I'm excited, Rudra..." Her enthusiasm was palpable. "I need to check if the waterproofing is done at the store, but I'll first go to the Airbnb I booked, keep my stuff there, and then head over to the store and meet the landlord. Where are you?"

"In the office... working for the Independence Day campaign," he replied, already rearranging his schedule to ensure he'd be free by six. A list of Thane's finest dining establishments had their websites open in six of his browser tabs.

"There's a slight change," she said, her tone tinged with a hint of apology. "My uncle called about an exhibition in the IIT Powai grounds. Could we have a late dinner? Say, around ten?"

"Late dinner is fine," Rudra responded, masking his disappointment. He wanted to spend as much time with her as possible.

"Are you sure?" The concern in her voice sounded genuine. "I can cancel too."

"No... no... don't compromise on your work," he insisted, pushing aside his selfish desire for a perfect evening. "This exhibition will help you with your work and networking." He told himself it was the right thing to do.

Throughout the day, their text exchanges continued until she casually mentioned visiting Sonakshi's place.

Sonakshi. The name felt familiar.

KK: Used to stay at Sonakshi's place before. For a decade. But now I don't. Sonakshi has this cat now as a pet. And I dislike that feline. That cat used to keep me worried while I slept. Also, I'm not too fond of cats.

RR: Even I'm not fond of them. I'm afraid of them.

KK: Hmmm....

RR: Have fun with Sonakshi. Perhaps you can go have lunch with her somewhere nearby.

Hours passed before her next message.

KK: Sonakshi is not well, is sleeping. Wbu?

RR: Am occupied with too much work as well... have a meeting in an hour.

After an unusually brief meeting, Rudra grabbed a power nap at his desk, dreaming about Kavya's beautiful smile. Some noise about flag distribution channels woke him up, but he looked around. There was nobody. He reached for his phone and saw that Kavya had sent no further message.

"Where are you?" he asked, concerned.

"Hey, I am working, will you call me later?" Something in her tone felt off, triggering a warning in his mind.

RR: What's the plan? Are we meeting after the exhibition?

KK: Very busy… if you want to see me, come to my Airbnb… we can chill there a little.

RR: If you're busy, you should finish your work… we can meet post the exhibition.

A growing unease settled in his stomach. Suddenly, her replies seemed distant. They had lost their warmth and excitement.

RR: Are you okay?

KK: errm… nothing… I just didn't like the salad I had, but the soup was pretty good.

RR: Order something else then.

KK: Not so sure… will eat something at the exhibition… I'm going there anyway… and if you wanna see me, we can catch up later.

As Rudra sat in his office, surrounded by campaign material, a hundred questions plagued his mind. Why was she acting strangely than usual? Was an ex-lover back in the picture? Or did she have a rival match on the dating app? Each question seemed more unsettling than the previous one. It felt challenging to reconcile this distant version of Kavya with the woman who'd shared intimate conversations with him only days before. He wasn't used to this unease… this feeling of not knowing.

Sonakshi's house carried the scent of lavender and something vaguely citrusy in the air. Kavya's nose wrinkled at it and looked around the carefully curated, minimalistic study. It was all clean lines and muted tones. This was quite different from the vibrant nature of her room back in her house at Nashik.

Kavya had known Sonakshi for more than a decade. They had grown up in the same locality, but after passing Grade 10, Sonakshi had moved to Mumbai. Despite the distance between them, they had kept in touch and stayed the best of friends. She could say that Sonakshi was her only best friend.

She often visited Sonakshi in the past, but of late, her visits had grown fewer. Though she came to the studio often, she hardly found time to visit her best friend, who stays in an apartment not far away. A few months had passed sincc she had come here last. Things felt a little different now.

Wearing a silk robe the colour of faded jade, Sonakshi reclined on a plush velvet sofa, a half-read book resting on her lap. A ginger tabby cat, Sonakshi had named Luna, curled up at her feet, its purr a low rumble. Kavya didn't like cats, and this Luna was the reason she didn't visit Sonakshi much. When Sonakshi would call Luna her soulmate, she would roll her eyes and make faces at her best friend. And if the cat saw her doing that, she would hiss even louder.

"Kavya!" Sonakshi said. "You had a date to go to, no?."

Kavya sat down on the soft-cushioned chair opposite her. "I did," she said, her eyes scanning the room. "Your cat seems to have grown, and you seem composed as ever. How are you feeling now, Sonakshi?"

"I'm doing well, thank you!" she replied. "And about my composure, well, I can't change that much now, can I? What about you? I hear you've been busy with your work… and some new… romantic interest?"

Kavya felt her cheeks flush, but she met her friend's gaze. "I'm doing great, and yes, I've been seeing someone. His name is Rudra."

Sonakshi's brows furrowed at the mention of his name. "Rudra… where do I know him from?" she wondered out loud.

Kavya giggled. "Not everyone I meet is someone you know or might have known, Sonakshi."

Sonakshi made a face at her and went back to reclining on her sofa. Meanwhile, Kavya felt her phone vibrate in her hand. Unlocking the phone, she read the notification. It was a message from Rudra. Her face softened into a smile at the message, something her best friend noticed.

"Oh, I see!" Sonakshi said. "He seems to be keeping you busy." She paused for a bit, perhaps waiting for Kavya to say something, and then added, "I'm so happy for you, you know."

Kavya nodded and was about to reply when her phone buzzed again. There was another text from Rudra.

She glanced at it, her fingers hovering over the screen, debating whether to reply to him immediately.

Sonakshi, however, was staring at her.

Kavya decided to put the phone back in her bag when a knock echoed through the hallway.

Sonakshi rose to her feet. "That must be him now," she teased. "I think you should finally introduce me to the man who has stolen my best friend's heart and time." She walked to the door, her jade-colored robe swirling around her.

Kavya followed closely behind, her heart doing a strange little dance in her chest.

Sonakshi opened the door to reveal Rudra, his hair dishevelled, his eyes betraying both surprise and shock. Kavya fidgeted where she stood, realising the sudden chill of tension in the air. She noticed Sonakshi staring at Rudra, and he returned hers with his own. It seemed as if she had stepped into a silent movie where everything was moving in slow motion.

"What happened?" she asked. "You both look as though you have seen each other's ghost."

Rudra's smile faltered while Sonakshi's face remained masked with a strange indifference.

She felt unease seeping into her, wondering if they knew each other somehow. Wasn't Sonakshi teasingly indicating just that moments ago? Why were they acting so weird with each other?

Neither had yet answered her question. The quiet made her uneasy.

"Rudra, this is my best friend, Sonakshi," Kavya said, her voice a little strained. "And Sonakshi, this is Rudra, the one with whom I have been going on dates."

"It's a pleasure to meet you, Sonakshi," Rudra said, although he extended no hand for her to shake. It seemed Sonakshi didn't mind either.

"Likewise, Rudra," Sonakshi replied, lacking any warmth.

She turned to Kavya, her gaze unwavering. "He's not at all like what you described him to be."

Kavya watched them with a knot of worry in her stomach. There was an undercurrent of tension she couldn't explain. A strange connection between them, she didn't understand. She tried to read their faces to catch what they were hiding, but they were quite good at not letting their true feelings show.

"What game are they playing?" she whispered to herself. "And why am I not invited to it?"

While posters featuring smiling politicians stared down from the walls, Rudra felt worried. The lunch date with Kavya had turned awkward with Sonakshi around. The same Sonakshi he had gone on a date with a few months ago. The same self-absorbed Sonakshi he had rejected and run out on. Why did she have to be Kavya's best friend?

The awkward encounter at Sonakshi's apartment kept playing in his mind. He had felt so disconcerted back there. All through the date afterwards, he was tense about whether she would tell Kavya about him. Not that she knew any secret about him, but he knew what kind of a girl she was.

Kavya, too, had picked up on the tension between the two. At one point, she had even asked them about their strange behaviour. He had kept quiet then and pretended to act normal, to play the polite suitor. Deep inside, though, he had been a mess.

Sonakshi had indirectly told him that she had fallen for him when she had caught him outside the restaurant. Today, she had constructed a facade of indifference at the lunch meeting.

He tried to focus on the endless spreadsheets and campaign strategies that littered his desk, but his mind kept drifting back to Kavya. He knew he liked her. There was a connection there he could not deny. It was unlike anything he had felt before.

Kavya was more than just a pretty face. She was intelligent, driven, and had a clear vision.

Hc genuinely believed he had met someone special and wasn't about to lose her to some bad blood from his past.

His phone buzzed that instant, interrupting his thoughts. Looking at the screen, he noticed Kavya had texted him.

KK: Had a good time. Sonakshi's cat was horrible, as expected.

He let out a small sigh of relief, realising that the world hadn't ended yet.

RR: Glad you had fun. You alright though?

His fingers played the desk like a drum as he waited for her reply. He wanted to ask her about Sonakshi, to know if she had mentioned something about him, but the rapid pounding of his heart kept him. From her message, Sonakshi had not her the truth yet. So, there was no need to disturb the status quo, but the thought of losing her over some past blunder made his stomach clench.

His phone buzzed again.

KK: Yes. Am good. Will sleep now.

Curiosity grew inside him, making him question why she had not asked him about Sonakshi again. At the date, she had been insistent about their weird behaviour. Right now, it looked as though she had forgotten it all. Perhaps he could leave it at that, but he didn't trust that Sonakshi would let the matter lie. He had seen her eyes at the restaurant, and those eyes glowed with jealousy and anger. He let out a frustrated sigh, questioning himself on how to deal with this situation.

He felt the need to act carefully but decisively. Years of experience campaigning and strategic manoeuvring kicked in. He needed to look at this as a problem he would usually face in political work. There was a problem; he needed a solution. And that too quickly. He had survived difficult campaigns before. He would survive this one, too.

Chapter 5

A Best Friend's Influence

KAVYA sat at her worktable, a half-finished embroidery in front of her. She should have been focusing on work, but the events of the previous afternoon occupied her mind. The awkward encounter between Sonakshi and Rudra kept flashing in front of her eyes. What had happened between them to act so weirdly with each other?

She had wanted Sonakshi to get along with Rudra. Instead, they acted awkwardly around each other, making her wonder if they knew each other from before. And if they did, had something bad happened between them? Only Rudra and Sonakshi could answer her question. Yet, she felt reluctant to ask, afraid that the truth would make her stumble.

Her phone buzzed.

She picked up her phone to see that Sonakshi had sent her a message.

Sonakshi: Morning! Hope you slept well. How are you feeling after last night?

Kavya hesitated. She wanted to be honest with Sonakshi and ask the question plaguing her mind. But instead of asking, she typed a different message.

Kavya: Morning. I'm good. A bit tired. What about you?

Within seconds, her phone buzzed again.

Sonakshi was calling this time.

Sliding the green phone icon upward, she answered the call. "Hey, Sonakshi. What's up?"

"Hey! Just wanted to check up on you," Sonakshi answered.

"Now that you had time to reflect… erm… how did you find Rudra?" Kavya kept her fingers crossed.

"He seemed very different from the way you described him, you know? A little… subdued."

Kavya frowned slightly. "He can be quiet at times, but he's very confident and smart. But I'm not sure what you mean by subdued." She wanted Sonakshi to actually tell her the truth about the awkwardness she shared with Rudra.

"Well, it's just that his career in politics…" Sonakshi began, her voice taking on a more critical tone. "It gives a certain kind of impression, no? Most of them are all the same, all about power and personal gain."

Kavya's eyebrows furrowed. "That's a very broad generalisation, Sonakshi," she replied, trying to keep her voice light. "Not everyone in politics is the same, and Rudra is not like that. He works hard and is dedicated to making a change. I would rather you did not judge him based on what others do."

"Maybe," Sonakshi conceded. "I'm just saying, sometimes appearances can be deceiving, right? And from the conversations we had, he seemed to be so different from what I expected, you know? Very intense."

"I like his intensity, and I'm pretty sure that he's very genuine and not putting up an act." She felt she should defend him.

"Okay, okay," Sonakshi chuckled, trying to lighten the mood. "I'm just saying that his political background might give the wrong impression, that's all. I'm sure he's a good person. But you need to be careful, no? People can be very manipulative, and you should not fall for it if he has any kind of bad intentions."

Kavya sighed. "I know how to be careful, Sonakshi," she said, trying not to show her frustration. "I can sense these things, and I'm capable of choosing my life partner. And anyway, Rudra is very different." She felt judged for being with someone her best friend didn't approve of. Sonakshi's words only confirmed my suspicion that all was not well between them.

"Okay, okay. I just want you to be happy," Sonakshi said softly, concerned. "You're my best friend, and I don't want to see you get hurt. And I don't want you to be with someone who you don't connect with."

She felt gratitude for Sonakshi's concern, but the latter's criticisms also irritated her. It was like her best friend's words were like poison to her ears, slowly infiltrating her thoughts.

She felt happy for Sonakshi's concern, but she wished that the latter would stop with her criticisms.

"Thanks, Sonakshi," Kavya said, feeling tired of this conversation. "I appreciate your concern. But I know what I'm doing."

"Of course you do," Sonakshi replied, her voice a bit too smooth. "Just remember that I'm here for you if you need anything." She added quickly, "So, what's up for the day? Are you going to work at the store?"

Kavya nodded, wanting to change the topic. "Yes, I've got a few things to do there, and then I'm working on an extensive project. So, I need to get going."

"Okay, then, you get going. Catch you soon?"

"Sure, bye Sonakshi," Kavya said as she hung up the call. Her fingers clenched around her phone. She wanted to know what happened between Rudra and Sonakshi. But should she ask?

Kavya had managed to stitch a few more lotus petals onto the silk fabric, but the thread felt unusually heavy in her hand. She was in the middle of unpicking a slightly crooked stitching when Rudra's name flashed on her phone's screen. Her heart, in that moment, did a small, involuntary skip. Was he going to tell the truth?

"Hey, Rudra," she greeted him as she answered the call.

"Hey, Kavya," he greeted her back. "Just wanted to check in on you. How's your day going?"

"It's okay," she replied. "Just catching up with work. How about you?"

"It's been a bit hectic," he said, sounding excited. "But I'm on my way to a new milestone."

"Oh, what happened?" She was genuinely curious.

"Well," Rudra began, enthusiastic, "I've been working on expanding my startups, you know? And I have some big news."

Kavya leaned back against her chair as he talked more about his two startups. He had told her he worked as a partner in a tech PR company and even opened a spiritual tourism venture with another person in the last few months. He did a lot of things and showed a lot of passion for it. "Tell me more."

"So, I've decided that my tech PR company, RaCe Communications, will cover more of the rural issues," he explained. "I want to use this platform to highlight the stories of the communities that live in the country's hinterlands and amplify their voices. And, as far as my spiritual tourism venture goes, I've decided to name it Yogic Pathways Travel Inc. My partner and I have shortlisted some spiritual centres and will be marketing them. These're not really that popular, you know. There are so many hidden gems out there."

As he went on about his plans and ambitions, Kavya listened without interrupting him. She admired his drive, his ambition, and his genuine desire to create a difference. She felt her attraction to him grow even more and would have surrendered to it had Sonakshi kept her words in check.

Power and personal gain. Personal appearances can be deceiving.

"That's amazing, Rudra," she said appreciatively. "Really commendable what you're doing."

"Thanks, Kavya," he said. "It's important to me that I do something meaningful, something that helps more than just me."

She appreciated that he was honest about what he was doing. But he was also doing a lot of things. The time he needed to give to his multiple businesses would be a lot. Would he have time for her?

"That's great," she said, her tone subdued. "But… how will you manage everything?" she asked, unable to keep the question to herself any longer.

Rudra paused. "It's a challenge, I won't deny it," he said. "But I'm passionate about what I do, and I have a great team. And I know how to manage my time."

Kavya nodded slowly, her fingers tracing the edge of her phone. "Well, I'm really proud of you," she said, her voice softening. "And I'm sure you'll manage everything."

"I hope so," he said, his voice warm. "You'll always be my motivation." He added, "Anyway, gotta get back to work. See you later, okay?"

"Sure. See you soon," she replied.

She placed her phone back on the table. She knew Rudra had the potential to do great work, but she was also worried about what all this might mean for their relationship.

A few hours later, Kavya found herself at a small café near Sonakshi's apartment, a place they had frequented often in the past. The smell of freshly brewed coffee filled the air.

Soon, Sonakshi arrived, her usual composed self.

"Hey," Sonakshi said, sliding into the chair across from Kavya. "What's up? You seem a bit distracted today."

Kavya took a sip of her coffee, considering how to phrase her thoughts. "I just spoke to Rudra," she began, "and he was telling me about how he's expanding his startups."

Sonakshi raised an eyebrow, her gaze sharp. "Oh, really? What's he expanding into now? To take over the world?"

A sigh escaped her mouth. "His tech PR firm is going into rural issues, and his spiritual tourism is looking into off-the-map spiritual places."

Sonakshi leaned back in her chair, her lips curving into a slight smile. "See? I told you," she said. "He seems more money-minded and ambitious than he lets on. He's doing so much, so how will he ever have the time for a proper relationship, Kavya?"

Kavya frowned. "He seems genuine, Sonakshi. And he said he knows how to manage his time."

Sonakshi laughed, a sharp sound. "That's what they all say. But relationships need time, Kavya. It's not about just saying a few sweet words. It's about being there, about spending quality time, about making the other person feel valued. And when you have so much on your plate, it's difficult to give enough time to someone." Sonakshi leaned forward, her gaze piercing. "And it feels like his actions are more about building his brand than actually caring for others."

Kavya decided not to answer. In fact, she worried that with all that was going on, would Rudra give her enough time?

Kavya's question wasn't entirely wrong. He himself wondered how he would manage time. On the call, he had conspired to show his best confidence. Deep inside, though, he was worried. Leaning against the wall, his mind focused on a solution to his quandary. His eyes completely ignored the comedy show playing on the television. He had reached the middle of a season, and usually he would laugh at the banter between the faces that had become familiar. But now the canned laughter of the show felt distant. With his mind in turmoil, he didn't notice that three episodes had passed. And, by the time the end credits rolled in, the clock blinked 2:30 A.M.

However, the question of time management was a smaller issue. The bigger one was what Sonakshi would eventually tell her. He asked himself why she hadn't yet done so, but should he wait for the self-absorbed narcissist to tell Kavya the truth? Shouldn't he be the one telling him? He wanted to call her right then, but he resisted the urge, knowing how much she valued her sleep.

Two more episodes blurred into a meaningless montage before exhaustion finally claimed him around half-past three.

Four hours of fitful sleep later, he woke with a dry throat and a heavy heart. He gulped down almost a litre of water, the cool liquid doing little to soothe the unease that had taken root in his chest. He reached for his phone, the screen flashing 7:55 A.M. He knew that Kavya was going to take a flight to Jamnagar for her exhibition.

RR: Reached the airport?

KK: Yes.

He could almost feel her distance, even in this brief text.

RR: Tell me... does this Sonakshi impact your life decisions?

He typed the message before he could talk himself out of it. He needed to know where her mind was at.

KK: No, but she's a close friend.

His chest tightened. He wanted her to be honest, but she wasn't giving him much to work with. He knew he had to push her, but he also didn't want to scare her away.

RR: You were very different yesterday.

There was a pause, a silent moment that stretched into what felt like an eternity, before her response appeared.

KK: Yes, I was... I tried to suppress my feelings... I was so consumed because of work, and it's my busy season. So, I was stressed.

His gut twisted. He knew she was busy; he also knew there was something else at play. He wasn't sure if it was just Sonakshi or something else.

RR: Okay, but it felt weird.

KK: Will call in a while. Checking in.

In the five-minute wait that followed, he told himself he needed to tell her the truth about what had happened between him and Sonakshi. Each minute of the wait felt like an eternity. Very soon, though, her name flashed on his phone screen. With a trepidating heart, he picked up the call.

"Kavya, I need to tell you something," he started without even the cursory hello. "About why I was awkward with your best friend."

"Okay…" That was all she would say as she waited for him to continue further.

"Sonakshi and I… well, we kind of went on a date… it was way before I met you… six months before, actually… and the date did not go well… I kind of ran out on her…" And he went on to describe what happened between him and Sonakshi on the date he had long wanted to forget and leave behind. He left out the part of what Sonakshi had told him at the date's end.

"Out of all the women in the world, you had to go out with my best friend, huh?" She sounded annoyed, but he had no answer to this. "You know," she continued, "Sonakshi and I have a WhatsApp group where we used to share the details of all the guys we used to date. Yours was missing, though."

He thanked God. "It was just an hour of small talk, that's it," he pleaded his innocence.

She fell quiet for a bit. He could only hear the faint sound of her breathing.

"Look, we both have our dating experiences," I said. "I won't deny that I have met more than twenty-five women through dating apps... and you must have gone out with other guys too... that's the past, and we shouldn't bother much..."

"I'll call you later," she said and ended the call.

The abrupt ending hurt him and made him feel guilty about telling her the truth. But there was no choice, really.

For four hours after, he wondered if he had lost her for good. He hoped not. She definitely was the one for him. He didn't want to let her go. At least not because of that, Sonakshi.

A year had passed since that horrible date. He had thought of it as a bad dream, but now it had turned into a nightmare. He wished he had never gone on that date. He wished that the wretched dating app had never matched him with Sonakshi.

He pondered whether he should call her again and pacify her. Just when he took out the phone to call her, she was already calling him. His heart leapt with joy as soon as he saw her name flash on the screen.

"Hello," he greeted, speaking into the phone. "Did you reach?"

"Yes… just now," Kavya said.

"Listen," he said, his voice gentle but firm, "I know you want exclusivity in all your life spheres, and I know you didn't feel exclusive after our talk a few hours ago. I understand the jealousy, but I've nothing to apologise for. It was the past, and it shouldn't decide our present or future." He paused, gathering his courage. "These days with you were full of exclusivity, honesty, and appreciation. I've started to like you, Kavya. I want us to grow into something meaningful." He knew he was being vulnerable and also knew it was something he had to do. He had to express his true feelings.

"Yes, Rudra, you're right," she said, "And yes, I felt all that you told me."

He felt his heart hammering against his ribs as he continued, "I haven't had this feeling for someone in a very long time. To be frank, I've never felt this way with any woman I've ever been with. You're different." His voice grew softer, a whisper almost. "I keep waiting for your texts. I couldn't sleep well last night… I waited until morning to text you."

She fell silent again. This time, though, there was more thought in it rather than tension. Even though she was beginning to feel vulnerable, he knew it.

"Rudra!" Her voice cracked slightly. He felt as though he had just won a battle, a battle that he was desperate to win. "You've broken my walls. I couldn't thank you more because if you hadn't called, I'd have always lived in suppression mode. I felt all you said, and yes, I too wish for this to grow into something meaningful."

"Thank you… now you should take some rest," he breathed.

"Rudra! Thanks for this conversation…"

"I was only being honest. Call me once you are better." His heart was still hammering, but now he had a sense of hope that things were on the right track.

When she called again in the evening, her voice carried a new warmth, the distance she had shown before now gone. "I thought mostly about our conversation," she admitted, "and now I feel confident about us."

Chapter 6

The Missing Inventory

RUDRA entered the office of RaCe Communications after a long time. The cabins and the desks felt a little different, though. Apparently, Celia Joseph, his partner, must have forgotten to apprise him of this change. She handled the day-to-day operations while he handled its matters remotely. His other work had not meant that he ignored what was happening here. He was in constant touch with the teams working here. Celia had told him recently she wanted the company to be revamped. He had suggested the idea for the company to cover rural issues. She had been reluctant at first, but he had insisted. Finally, she agreed to his plans. The good thing was that Celia trusted him with this.

The day's plans plastered the various screens and whiteboards scattered throughout the office. Most of the screens' headlines were about a transport strike that started a couple of days ago, leading up to a state-wide shutdown. The state media clamoured for information from an unusually quiet government. Staring at the headlines, Rudra decided to use this moment to elevate RaCe's status in the industry. He did not want to just report the news, but to give shape to a narrative, to give voice to those who were often overlooked. His team had been working on his wishes since the early hours of the day. The freelancers he had hired were in the field, capturing the raw emotions and the frustrations of the protestors.

His lead associate, Gulnaaz Ahmed, approached him with a tablet in hand.

Contrary to most women in her community, Gulnaaz had dyed her hair pink, did not care much for the maulanas' diktats, and had publicly proclaimed herself as an atheist. Her community considered her a rebel, but it had not mattered to her. She had even separated herself from her family. He had not directly asked her, but the office grapevine carried a lot of gossip around.

Professionally, he trusted her judgment. She did stellar work and handled much of his work here at the company. Without her, it would have been difficult for him to manage the company affairs.

"Rudra Sir, we have the first cut of the coverage ready," she said, her voice slightly breathless. "Check this out, it's incredible."

Rudra took the tablet and noticed the screen filled with powerful images of the drivers on strike. They looked angry and determined. There were videos of their raw and unfiltered sloganeering as well. A surge of pride raced inside him, satisfied with what his team had captured.

"Wow," he breathed out, his gaze fixed on the screen. "This is… this is powerful, Gulnaaz. This is exactly what we needed."

"Right?" Gulnaaz grinned, excited. "We've got interviews, footage, and some really compelling stories. We just need to finalise the angles for distribution."

Rudra nodded, his mind already racing. "Okay, let's gather the team. I want to finalise the messaging and discuss our distribution strategy." He clapped his hands, making others in the office turn towards him. "Team, let's assemble. We have a story to tell."

Oh, how he wished Celia were here! But she had gone to attend a family function. Her sister-in-law had given birth to a baby girl.

Writers, designers, and strategists made up most of the team at RaCe Communications. At his call, they all gathered around the table in the conference room, every one of them as excited as he was.

"Okay," Rudra began, his voice strong and clear. "We have some powerful footage and stories from the protest. Now we need to decide how we're going to present it to the world. Gulnaaz, what are your initial thoughts on our lead?"

Gulnaaz stepped forward, her pink hair bouncing slightly as she spoke. "I think we need to focus on the human aspect, Rudra Sir. The plight of these drivers, their struggles, the sacrifices they're making. We need to make people understand that this is not just about traffic jams and insanely high tolls, but about real people fighting for their rights."

"I agree," Rudra said, his eyes scanning the team. "But we also need to highlight the injustice, the exorbitant tolls that are pushing these people to the brink. We need to make it clear that this is a systemic issue, not just a local problem."

"What about our social media strategy, Rudra Sir?" asked Satya, his social media strategist, always the one to be on top of the trending topics. "How do we ensure that this message reaches the right audience?"

"We need to use all our platforms, Satya," Rudra replied, his eyes glinting with determination. "Twitter, Instagram, Facebook, and every other platform we can get our hands on. We need to make this story viral. Use the hashtag 'HighwayJusticeNow' and make sure the graphics are powerful, visually strong."

"And let's not forget our traditional PR channels," said Priya, her public relations expert. "Let's draft a press release highlighting the key takeaways and distribute it to all our contacts in the media."

Rudra nodded, feeling proud of his team. "Okay, let's get to work, people… this is our chance to make a difference. This is RaCe's moment."

As his team dispersed, he moved and looked out the window at the bustling city below. His eyes subconsciously moved northward and a little west, his mind wondering how Kavya was doing.

Kavya entered the exhibition hall to find a lot of hammering and drilling around her. The hall thrummed with a vibrant energy that fueled her excitement. Workers animatedly chatted with each other, their supervisors barking orders and snapping at them to work faster. Colourful banners fluttered from the rafters, their bold hues swaying under the glaring spotlights. The air hung heavy with sawdust, prickling her skin as she wove through the hustle. Her heart thudded in her chest, its frequency trying to match the surrounding clatter.

She stopped before her own modest stall. It stood half-assembled, skeletal display racks jutting out like bare bones. Boxes of colourful fabrics she had brought from Mumbai lay stacked, their contents still inside, waiting to be displayed. Her breath hitched as she counted the boxes.

Only half her inventory had arrived. There was a sinking feeling in her heart that the rest wouldn't make it before the exhibition opened for the public tomorrow.

Her hand raked through her hair, panic pulsing through her. She'd pictured a stall full of her finest sarees and silks. Now, with half of her vision missing, it felt like the universe was laughing at her.

"Lokesh, any word from the transporter?" she asked, voice taut.

Lokesh, his brow furrowed in concern, shook his head. "No, Kavya Madam. I've called him a dozen times, but his phone's dead. It's like he's dropped off the face of the earth."

Kavya sighed, a knot of unease forming in her stomach. She glanced at her phone, a text from Rudra still unread, showing on the screen. It was a lifeline she ached to grab, but couldn't bring herself to touch. "Pradnya, what about the unpacking?"

Pradnya looked up from the pile of fabrics she was arranging, her hands pausing mid-motion.

"I've done what I can, Kavya Madam, but it's only half of what we planned."

Kavya took a deep breath. "Alright. Let's call the artisans directly. Maybe they've a workaround," she said. She scrolled through her contacts and decided to start with Padma Tajanpure, an old hand at making the most intricate designs, who worked in the northern hinterlands near Bhusawal. She dialled her number and waited for the lady to pick up.

"Padma ji, it's Kavya, how are you?" Kavya asked, trying to keep her tone light.

A pause stretched across the line before Padma answered. "Kavya beta, we're so sorry. We tried everything to get your pieces to you, but the transport strike... It's chaos here. The unions have dug in, and no one's budging."

She felt her stomach plummet. "The drivers are still blocking the highways?"

"Yes, beta," Padma replied. "It's a deadlock. Only emergency vehicles are allowed through. We even reached out to private transporters, but they're all siding with the strikers. There's no way around it."

Frustration flared in her chest. "But, Padma ji, this is my livelihood! I've got half my inventory here. HALF! How am I supposed to stand out with just this?"

"I know, beta," Padma replied, her tone sympathetic. "We're heartsick over it. We pushed every limit we could, but the strike's got us trapped."

Kavya ended the call, the phone slipping slightly in her damp grip. The news of the strike had been blaring for days, but she had not thought that it would hurt her business. It was the reason her stall was half-empty. She stared at the dull and uninspired content in the boxes. These were supposed to be her backup. Without her signature designs, her stall risked fading into the sea of cut-throat competitors.

Why her? Why was the universe so intent on turning against her dreams? Why did it not want her to carve her name in this ruthless industry? After everything she had done, a strike threatened to undo her efforts. Without half her inventory, she would not make her profits. And without the profits, she couldn't clear the loans she had taken or pay salaries to her employees.

Kavya shoved her despair back, locking it behind gritted teeth. She was not going to break now. Her shoulders squared, she turned to face Lokesh and Pradnya, who watched her with wide, anxious eyes.

But now, she had to do something. She had to make do with what she got.

She would not let a transport strike destroy her dreams. She wanted to be a popular fashion entrepreneur and designer, and she would become one.

"We'll make do with what we've got," she told her assistants. "Let's arrange these fabrics. We can also perhaps weave a story about them, something to hook the visitors."

Pradnya's face softened. "We could play up the colours and textures. Erm… build a theme around them?"

Lokesh nodded. "And the empty spaces… well, we could fill them with sketches or props or something."

Kavya's lips curled into a faint smile. "Exactly… it's not everything, but enough to make a mark."

A strike will not bury her dreams, she told herself. She was going to rise above it, stitch by stubborn stitch.

Rudra sank into the stiff leather chair, the long polished table before him set like a chessboard primed for war. An array of government officials sat before him, all of them hardened negotiators, their faces strong like granite. Even though he had grown up among the political crowd, he could discern nothing from their posture. At thirty-two, he was the youngest there, plucked from the volunteers because of his past activism.

The door swung open with a loud creak, revealing the approach of three men, their steps reverberating across the chamber like a thunderclap on stone. He knew them on sight. They were the vanguard of the transport union. Aslan Shaikh led the trio, his face a mask of weathered lines and piercing eyes. Bhuria Yadava, a man with a burly frame, followed him, and the last, a young man named Ganesh Bahutale, the most volatile and unpredictable of the lot.

They took their seats at the table, their eyes roving about the others and settling on him at last. They seemed to ask him, "What's a greenhorn like you doing here?" But he held their stares, refusing to flinch. The outcome of this meeting would decide the resolution of the protests.

Mr Sharma, a recently inducted government official but high in the party's ranks, broke the silence with a rasp like dry leaves. His brows were always furrowed, no matter the situation. "Gentlemen, thank you for joining us," he said, his tone threaded with a faint quiver. "We recognise the gravity of the situation and are here to hear you out."

Aslan Shaikh leaned forward. "We didn't come to trade pleasantries, Mr Sharma," he snarled, gravelly. "We've been shouting into the void for years. Now we're here to claim what we deserve."

Bhuria dipped his head, his gaze intense. "Our people are breaking their backs. Their families are going hungry. We're done waiting for scraps."

Ganesh pounded his fist on the table, its sound like a gunshot. "How long do we let you drain us? When does it stop?"

Rudra felt his pulse quickening as their words washed over him. Their fury he understood too well. He'd walked their picket lines, seen the toll booths perched like vultures on every road, and watched their families ration hope as costs gnawed at their lives. They had complained before, but the government's machinery moved slowly. Hulking. Sluggish. Clogged with procedure despite the recent overhauls. The elections loomed ahead. Failure here could undo everything the party and the government had worked for.

He saw Mr Sharma blanch.

"We hear your grievances," Mr Sharma teetered, his fingers tightening around his pen. "But we need a full picture. Tell us what you're asking for."

Aslan's gaze didn't waver. "Cut the tolls. The rates are choking us, and we need relief. Elections are breathing down your neck. Fix this or watch the fallout."

"Damn right!" Bhuria remarked, fists clenched.

"We'll clog every road, strangle every route until we get what's fair," Ganesh's voice slashed through.

The officials shifted in their seats, their chairs creaking under the mounting pressure.

Rudra felt the room tighten, almost like a bowstring close to snapping. This wasn't how negotiations took place. The protest leaders were outright blackmailing the government.

Mr Sharma cleared his throat again, a sharp tug reeling Rudra's back.

"What if we ease the strain first?" he said, calm but firm. "A temporary toll cut to buy time while we hammer out the rest?"

Aslan's probing eyes focused on him. "And what keeps you from stalling once the spotlight dims?"

Rudra didn't blink. "We tie it to deadlines. Very public deadlines. You watch us deliver."

Bhuria snorted. "Talk's easy. We need something ironclad."

"Then we make it ironclad," he snapped. "A committee is evenly split. Your people. Our people. Tracking every move."

"You expect us to believe that you'll play straight?" Ganesh's mouth twisted.

"No," Rudra said. "I expect you to hold us accountable. This is the first step. We build from here."

Silence greeted the chamber.

The union leaders traded glances while Mr Sharma's eyes darted to him, gratitude evident.

Aslan nodded slowly. "We'll chew on it, but we don't budge until we see results."

Rudra let out a breath. It wasn't a win. Not yet. But surely some ground had been gained. For now, this would do.

Chapter 7

Independence Day Speech

THE 15th of August unfurled like a banner. Under the morning sky, Rudra stood backstage, watching the culmination of weeks of tireless efforts by his fellow workers. They had worked on the Ghar Ghar Tiranga campaign with great energy. He had seen its result on his drive here. Tricolour flags hoisted on balconies, staffs jutting proudly from window sills. The sight of each one had strengthened the anticipation in his chest. This wasn't just a ceremony. It was his chance to reach people and to stoke the embers of their hope.

Outside, the ground behind the party thrummed with life. Saffron, white and green banners snapped in the breeze, their edges frayed from the wind's eager tugging. Marigolds spilt across tables and dangled in garlands, their earthy scent cutting through the muggy heat. Volunteers wove through the throng, shouting 'Jai Hind!' at the top of their voices. Posters with 'Happy Independence Day' written in bold black letters clung to every wall and post. People gathered here possessed a fervour cracking like static before a storm. All eyes were fixed on the empty podium, waiting.

Rudra's lips moved as he rehearsed his speech. He'd drafted every word with care, sanding down platitudes until only the raw truth remained. The speech he was going to give would not be about politics or posturing. It was about connection, about reminding the people of the nation they shared. His fingers brushed the hem of his crisp white kurta, his eyes flickering to his phone. Kavya's unread message lingered there, making him want to read it. But that could wait. He slid the phone back into his pocket.

A senior party leader, Mr Sadanand Patil, who always wore a stern expression on his face, approached him. "Rudra beta, it is time," he said. "Are you ready?"

Rudra nodded, taking a deep breath. "Yes, Patil Saheb, I'm ready."

He stepped forward, the world flaring into chaos in front of him. Spotlights momentarily blinded him, white-hot and unrelenting, while the crowd's roar slammed into him. His boots sank into the carpeted stage, his eyes scanning the eager, expectant, motley crowd. His stomach lurched as he noticed too many eyes on him. But he'd volunteered for this, hadn't he? He had pushed through the pressure and spent many sleepless nights on this.

He adjusted the microphone, took another deep breath, and began, "My dear fellow citizens, today we don't just mark our freedom. We honour the blood and grit of those who carved it. Those who dreamed of a nation stitched together by unity, justice, and equality."

He paused for a moment, letting his words sink in.

"But let's not hide from the truth," he continued. "Our nation's scars still weep. Inequality gnaws at us, a hunger that spares no corner. Injustice doesn't whisper. It stalks, bold and unashamed, through our streets and homes. "

A ripple stirred the crowd.

"We're at a fork in the road," he declared, pressing on. "One path keeps progress locked in gilded cages, dangled just out of reach. The other throws the gates wide open. A path we must take. It's a country where the farmer bent over his plough, the artisan threading her loom, the kid kicking dust in some village lane, all get an equal shot. Not scraps, but a real stake."

The crowd listened to him with rapt attention now.

"We're a nation of makers, of voices. Our past isn't dead weight. It's the soil we grow from. Let's plant something new where tradition and tomorrow don't just coexist but fuel each other."

His words flowed like a smooth river finding its course. He could feel the shift in the crowd, see their eyes lit up.

"We need a nation that doesn't flinch from change," he urged. "A place where spiritual tourism isn't just a slogan but a bridge to our roots. Where technology doesn't divide us but stitches us closer, helping us solve the riddles of hunger, of fairness, of forgotten voices."

He then wove in stories he'd gathered. The farmer whose hands cracked like the earth he tilled. The weaver whose patterns held generations of unsung pride. He brought their stories alive with his words, making the crowd feel the stories rather than just hearing them.

"So, let's swear to it," he said, "to build a nation that's free down to its bones, just in its blood, equal in its heartbeat. Let's link hands and drag our dreams into the light. Jai Hind!"

As he spoke, he felt a sense of purpose in what he was doing. He felt proud of his work here, in the impact he was making. He knew he wasn't perfect, but he was trying to be a better version of himself every day.

"Let us, therefore, recommit ourselves to building a nation that is truly free, truly just, and truly equal. Let us work together, hand in hand, to make our dreams a reality. Jai Hind!"

Applause filled the air, a roar that rattled the stage beneath him. His chest heaved, pride surging hot and bright. He felt happy to have reached them, hoped he'd cracked through their apathy, and let something real spill out. A grin tugged at his lips as he stepped back. The dancers swept in behind him, skirts flaring like blossoms caught in a gust, but he barely noticed.

Kavya's heels tapped against the scuffed wooden flooring of a small conference room she had booked to meet the artisans who worked with her. She'd missed Rudra's Independence Day function for this. Guilt gnawed at her for rejecting his invitation. But this meeting was important as well. The scent of sweet jasmine incense and the faint musk of worn fabric laced the air. Sunlight gleamed in through the grimy windows.

She decided to send him a voice note after a lot of negotiation with herself.

Hey Rudra…I decided to just send you a voice note instead of texting you. Listen, I am really, really sorry about not making it to your speech. I know it was important to you, and I know I said I'd come, but it has been…well…tricky here. This meeting was very important too. I am so sorry, and I'll make it up to you. See you later?

Padma Tajanpure sat near the front with her hands nestled in her lap, her eyes showing the gathered wisdom from her years of struggle. Beside her sat Leela Sachdev, her fingers fidgeting with the hem of her saree, her forehead creased as though suspicious of her new surroundings. To Padma's left was Karan Vij. He slouched against the back wall with crossed arms, defiant. Now, their gazes fell on her, making her squirm.

"Thank you all for meeting me today," she said with a shallow breath. "I know the past few weeks have been challenging. The new government policies have piled onto existing challenges. We're all suffering because of that."

"We've been drowning for years, Kavya beta. No one's ever pulled us up. What can you do now?"

Leela nodded. "We've clung to dreams, hoping there will be a change, but it's like grasping at air. Now, more challenges rise against us."

Kavya took a deep breath, her heart pounding against her ribs. "I feel you," she said, softening her tone. "Things are grim, but we can't let that bury us. Government policies, we cannot do much about, but maximising our revenue, we can do something about."

She paused, her gaze meeting the eyes of each artisan in the room. "I've been working on something. A platform called Artisan Connect. It'll be a digital space where you can directly share your work, sell straight to buyers, and keep what's rightfully yours. No middlemen siphoning your sweat." She leaned into her words more. "Imagine this… your own profiles, your stories told your way. Higher payouts, wider reach, control over your craft and future."

A moment of silence followed her speech.

A younger artisan, a man named Karan Vij, spoke up. "That sounds good, Kavya Madam, but digital space is not exactly easy to understand for most of us rural folks."

"What do you propose, then?" she asked.

"Rural artisans need to be educated. And this will not be a straightforward task, you know. Our education system does not favour us, and it will be a bureaucratic hassle to change education norms."

"Surely we can achieve all this by simply teaching computers and how to operate the Internet for the time being?" she posited. "We find partners with the government's Digital India initiative and have their people educate you all while I focus on my business model and get this platform up and running. But until then, I also plan to launch a social marketing campaign that will hopefully exploit the digital space to sell more of your products. Exhibitions can only do so much."

A murmur of agreement swept through the room.

"That's good to hear, beta," Padma Tajanpure spoke up. "But as long as these truck protests persevere, any logistics will be difficult to handle."

She sighed. The transport strike was really an issue. She hoped the government would engage with them successfully and bring an end to the protests.

As she walked out, she heard a ping on her phone. It was Rudra; he'd sent a voice note. She braced herself as she played it.

Kavya, I know this meeting was important to you. I totally get it. You don't have to make up to me; there is nothing to make up for. The speech went great, I'll tell you all about it. I wish you were here, though. Tell me how the meeting went later? See you very, very soon.

Kavya sighed. This was indeed a sweet, sweet man.

Chapter 8

It's Happening

HAPPY with how things had turned out with Rudra, Kavya returned to her Airbnb room in Mumbai and sat on the edge of her bed. His unwavering support had made her feel better and managed to soothe her frayed nerves. He was like a gentle balm to her weary soul.

She had always been fiercely independent, always relied on her own strength, but now she couldn't deny the powerful pull of her emotions. She was beginning to feel something real, something deep for Rudra. She had always been careful, always guarded her heart, but with Rudra, she felt a sense of freedom, a feeling that she could truly be herself. It was as though he was capable of breaking down her walls, all the walls she had built over the years.

She picked up her phone, her fingers hovering over Sonakshi's name. She knew she had to talk to her. She had to share what she was feeling. It wasn't easy to admit these things to someone she was not entirely sure about. She still remembered the things Sonakshi had told her about Rudra, but she chalked it off to jealousy. She knew Sonakshi was a good friend, but she was also worried about her reaction.

She called Sonakshi, her heart doing a nervous flip as she waited for her to answer.

"Hey, Kavya, what's up?" Sonakshi's voice was smooth and calm, as always. "You sound a bit different today."

"Hey, Sonakshi," Kavya said, trying to keep her voice light and casual, as if she had not just made a life-changing decision. "I just wanted to talk to you about something."

"Okay, sure. What is it?" Sonakshi asked, and there was a little more attention in her tone.

Kavya took a deep breath before speaking her thoughts out loud. "I am… I am starting to love Rudra," she said, the words feeling both vulnerable and liberating. "It's… it's a weird feeling. It's as though I've never felt this way before."

There was a moment of silence on the other end.

She felt an anxious knot tightening her stomach, unsure of what Sonakshi's reaction was going to be.

"Oh!" Sonakshi finally remarked, her voice carefully measured. "That's… interesting."

Kavya frowned, her heart sinking. "What do you mean by 'interesting'?" she asked, sounding defensive all of a sudden.

"I just mean, you know, you've always been so careful, so guarded," Sonakshi said, her tone still carefully neutral. "And this seems like a big step for you."

Kavya nodded, her fingers now trembling slightly. "It is a big step for me. But it also feels right." She paused, then added, "And I'm going to wait for him to propose to me. I know it sounds silly, but I want him to be the one to make that decision. That's what I have always imagined."

Sonakshi let out a small laugh, both dismissive and patronising. "Oh, Kavya, you're being so naïve," she said. "You should not pin your hopes on him. I still think that he's not the right man for you, you know? He's too ambitious, too focused on his career, on making a name for himself. And he's too much of a politician."

Kavya's eyebrows furrowed, a surge of anger rising within her. "Sonakshi, stop," she said, her voice now sharp. "I'm not naïve. I'm making my own choices. And I don't want you to talk about him like that. You don't know him the way I do."

"But, Kavya, I'm just looking out for your best interests," Sonakshi said. "I don't want to see you get hurt. You deserve better than him." She was sounding more serious now, her tone revealing how bothered she was by this entire conversation.

"And I'm telling you, Sonakshi, that you should stay away from commenting on my personal relationships," Kavya said, her voice now rising slightly. "I know that you're my friend, but it's my life, and I know what I want. And right now, I want to be with Rudra."

"But Kavya…" Sonakshi began, her voice now pleading. "I just… I can't see you with him. He's not the kind of person you need."

"And you should also stop talking like you know what kind of person I need!" Kavya retorted, her voice now full of anger. "This is my life, and I will choose my own partner. You should just stay out of it." Why was Sonakshi being so critical of being with Rudra? What could have possibly happened on that one date that Sonakshi had developed such a negative view of him?

"I'm only telling you this because I care about you, Kavya," Sonakshi said, her voice now softer. "I'm only looking out for your best interests. You have been like a sister to me, and I can't help but be worried about you."

"Thanks for your concern, Sonakshi," Kavya said, her voice flat. "I appreciate it, but please respect my decision. I have made up my mind."

"Fine," Sonakshi said, her tone now cold. "If that's what you want, I won't say anything else. But when he breaks your heart, don't come crying to me."

Kavya ended the call, her heart heavy, wishing she had never called her.

The small, cosy cafe felt like heaven on earth as the aroma of freshly brewed coffee wafted in his nose. Rudra slouched at the corner table, its chipped wood edges worn smooth by countless elbows, and eyed his friends across the steaming mugs between them. Ashutosh Karmalkar sprawled in his seat, one arm flung over the back of his chair with a wide grin on his face. His other friend, Shailesh Mehta, sat straighter, fingers tapping on the table.

Both looked as exhausted as he was.

Rudra lifted his mug and took a sip of his bitter coffee. An image of Kavya lingered in his mind, her voice playing like a stuck reel. He flexed his fingers around the ceramic, resisting the urge to call and meet her.

"So," he began, his voice casual, "how'd you two survive without me?"

Ashutosh grinned, being the most jovial one in the group. "Survive? Dude, we thrived. Threw a proper rager the other night. Pity you were off in Nashik playing dutiful son."

Shailesh nodded. "Office was all okay, too. But it's duller without you stirring the pot. What about you? Nashik wear you down?"

Rudra shrugged, dodging their eyes. "It was good. Parents are solid. Just…tired, I guess."

His phone buzzed against his thigh. Kavya's name flashed on the screen when he took it out. His pulse tripped at it.

He let it sit unanswered, though.

"Look, I've got something on my mind. I need your advice."

Their gazes sharpened.

Ashutosh leaned in, elbows thudding the table. "Oh, let me guess… starts with an 'M', ends with a heart attack? Spill it, Rudra."

"Yeah, alright. Kavya. She's… I don't know… she's different. Everything clicks with her."

Shailesh raised his brows. "Clicks how? Paint us a picture, lover boy."

His fingers tightened on the mug, his knuckles whitening. "It's like… I don't have to fake it with her. She sees the raw, messy me, and I want to be there, you know? Catch her when she stumbles." He exhaled hard. "I think I'm falling for her. Properly falling."

Ashutosh whooped, slapping the table so hard the mugs on it rattled, while Shailesh whistled triumphantly. Their laughter ricocheted off the cafe's walls, drawing the curious stares of the people around. Rudra winced, ducking his head as his cheeks blazed, embarrassed.

"Finally!" Ashutosh crowed, jabbing a finger at him. "We've been betting on when you'd realise it, you idiot."

Shailesh chuckled. "You've dodged feelings like they're tax collectors. About time you got hit in the chest."

Rudra's cheeks flushed again. "Easy, I'm still figuring it out. She's got a lot on her plate. Don't even know if she's on the same page as me."

"Figuring it out?" Ashutosh snorted, leaning back with a theatrical groan. "Rudra, you're a politician. Stop campaigning and start confessing. She's the one, right?"

"She is," he admitted. "But what if I mess it up? What if she's not ready?"

"Dude," Shailesh cut in, "you're circling like a vulture. She's not a policy to debate. Just tell her. Do something big."

His brow creased. "Big like what?"

"Propose!" Ashutosh suggested, mockingly, his grin taking on a feral note. "Sweep her off her feet before some other guy does. You're not getting younger, and she's not gonna wait forever."

Shailesh nodded. "Love's not a boardroom deal. Quit strategising and jump. What are you so afraid of?"

His jaw slackened. "Propose? You're having a laugh."

"I am being serious," Ashutosh shot back. "You're mad for her, she's mad for you, why hesitate? Pop the question."

"Yup," Shailesh agreed. "Stop playing chess with your heart. Be the man who shows up, not the one who plans forever."

His thoughts spun. He pictured Kavya in his mind, and the ache in his heart sharpened. They were right. What was he waiting for? Some grand signal? Permission slips from the universe?

"I… maybe you're right," he muttered, "but the timing feels off. She's swamped with her own mess."

Ashutosh rolled his eyes. "Timing's never perfect, genius. You love her? Then quit stalling before she's someone else's."

Shailesh gripped his shoulders. "Overthinking's always been your negative point, Rudra. Trust what you feel. Go get her."

Their words made the knot in his stomach unravel. He couldn't keep on hiding his feelings this way. Kavya's answer might be a mystery to him, but for once, he'd leap. Whatever came next, he'd face it head-on.

"Alright!" he said. "I'll do it. I'll propose."

Chapter 9

Finally, He Proposed!

RUDRA stepped into a vibrant restaurant just on time. Being late had always been his habit, but not tonight. Not with Kavya waiting. He'd bathed twice today deliberately. He didn't want any sign of the day's grit to linger on his body. He'd arrayed himself in a light blue shirt striped with white, sleeves rolled twice to bare the glint of his golden-brown watch, and cream linen trousers. A brown pen rested in his chest of drawers.

He spotted her across the room, a silhouette under the ageing lamp. Her dark shirt clung to her body, the delicate hook at her neck catching the amber light. Loose, bluish linen pyjamas covered her legs. A half-embroidered jacket draped her shoulders. Her silver bunstick gleamed, pinning her hair into a crown, and the mascara framing her eyes deepened their pull. But it was the mole on her nose that held his gaze more.

He growled low, making her jolt in her seat. A flash of irritation passed in her eyes. "Rudra!" she snapped and then softened. Her scowl melted into a grin. She proferred a handshake, which he accepted, his fingers grazing hers. The touch lingered for a moment, electric and heavy. Their dynamic had shifted.

She called the waiter, requesting water for herself, before asking, "What will you have?"

He sank into the leather couch, savouring the wide curl of her lips, sweet and unguarded. His own grin faltered like a clumsy echo. To him, she seemed like a mirage, and yet she was real.

"You're staring," she accused mockingly.

"Can't help it," he shot back. "You look like you stepped out of a dream."

She laughed. "And you're laying it on thick tonight."

He smirked, shrugging. "Truth doesn't need layers."

The waiter arrived just then, and Kavya ordered water and arched a brow at him. "Your turn. What'll it be?"

"Surprise me," he said, his grin daring her.

She rolled her eyes but was definitely amused. "Fine, but no whining later."

She'd always known his tastes. He liked bold, spicy food. He trusted her to wield that knowledge. The waiter returned with a towering plate of nachos, cheese dripping over jalapenos, and together they dove in, fingers brushing over the same chip. She laughed yet again, slicing through the knot in his chest.

"Gin, 60ml with water," she told the waiter.

"Chivas 18, 30ml, water," he countered.

"Aglio olio spaghetti," she said.

"And a hummus platter," he added.

"How was the drive?" he asked after the waiter left.

"Slept half the way," she answered, stretching slightly. "We dropped Mihir off at a friend's place in Vasai. He tags along with me sometimes to meet his friends."

"And the shoot prep?"

"Locked in," she replied. "All planned."

"Where's your driver?" he frowned, scanning the room as though the man might appear.

"Sent him back." Her eyes met his. "Knew you'd take me home."

A thrill curled in his gut, quickening his pulse. He was already looking for the drive ahead.

"Plants," she said suddenly. "Do you like them?"

"Love them," he answered. "Gardens are my morning ritual. Back in Nashik, I'd walk mine every day."

Her face lit up, wistful. "I want a house full of them—living room, bedroom, balcony. Green everywhere."

"Mine'd have a big garden," he said. "Vintage stuff too. Old furniture. Carved wood. A mix of history and roots."

The spaghetti soon arrived.

With her deft hands, she served him a portion and then put the rest into her plate. They ordered another round of drinks soon after the hummus arrived.

After they finished off the hummus, he asked, "Still hungry?"

She shook her head. "Spaghetti's enough."

His stomach growled, so he ordered a cottage cheese steak, timing it for after their third round. The clock crept past eleven, then midnight. Their cigarettes dwindled as well. He waved at the waiter. "Can you grab more?"

"Shops are shut," the man replied, apologetic.

Kavya smirked. "Quit like a cold turkey, Rudra."

He squinted. "What?"

"Means you finish that one and never touch another," she said, eyes glinting. "Right then and there."

He chuckled, smoke curling from his lips. "Maybe tomorrow."

Their fourth drinks landed, the steak alongside, but his hunger had faded.

Her voice rose, singing softly. He joined her with his rough and off-key voice, stumbling over 'mere saamne waali khidki main' and 'aapki nazron ne samjha.'

A staff member coughed.

They drained their water glasses. Rudra stood after, offering his hand.

Hers slipped into his, fingers clasping each other tight. The side hug came quick and electric, and they stepped into the night outside, hand in hand, the cool air sharp against their faces.

In the car, silence pressed at them.

Rudra drove slowly on purpose. The Airbnb was only a couple of kilometres away, so he didn't want to end the drive fast. He kept stealing glances at her reflection in the rearview mirror.

"Kavya," he started in a ragged voice. "I can't keep this in. I've said I like you, but it's more. It's different. I love you. Never felt this before, but you're a part of me. Shree Krishna gave me this. Gave me you. And I can't imagine losing it… losing you."

He gripped her hands as the car rolled to a stop outside her Airbnb.

Her face flushed, eyes glassy. "Turn off the AC," she murmured. And then her voice turned louder. "Rudra, I love you too. I've fallen… hard… and it's real. You're my best friend, my everything. I thought I'd never let myself feel this, but with you, it's mature. It's right. It's you who I've been waiting for."

He kissed her hand, lips brushing her knuckles. They hugged and locked themselves in that position for a few moments, but he pulled back and kissed her forehead. The kiss was slow and tender, a fuse finally aflame.

"Inside?" she whispered, breath warm against his jaw.

"The owner—," he began, hesitant.

"Won't care," she cut in, mischief glinting in her eyes.

He followed her into the Airbnb, her bold stride pulling him deeper in. It was something he surrendered to.

The door snapped shut behind them, and they soon embraced again, melding into each other, arms tangling. His pulse thundered, hammering in sync with hers. A fierce duet he'd never heard before. This feels like home, he thought. A silent prayer slipped past his lips.

They took their act to the bed, his eyes tethered to hers. A grin broke across his face, mirrored in hers, and their lips closed in enough to land a pucker. The air between them cackled with warmth.

Words and laughter followed in the night after. They painted their future in bold strokes. A wedding. Kids tumbling through their vivid dream house. Rudra, who'd always dodged plans as though they were stray bullets, found himself plotting his future with her.

"No dancing at the wedding," he announced, a smirk tugging at his lips.

She laughed. "Good thing I'm picturing a quiet temple affair. No room for a dance floor anyway."

They sank deeper into the bed, her head nestled in the crook of her arm.

"Hot water?" he asked.

She nodded, peeling away to spark the kettle to life. As it rumbled, she turned and smiled. "Every time you walk through the door, I'll have it ready."

His chest tightened. She was already dreaming of a blissfully married life with him, further than he was.

They sipped from their glasses, steam spiralling into the air.

"Let's grab some sleep, bro," he said, feeling exhausted.

She scrunched her nose. "Bro? Seriously?" And then, quieter, "I've got a shoot at six."

"Six?" His brows shot up. "You didn't say that."

"Shoots always kick off at dawn," she teased.

His eyes flicked to the clock. It was 3 A.M. now.

"Cruel, I thought we had till sunrise."

They curled back into each other, her fingers sketching lazy trails across his palm. Sleep took them soon enough, but the smiles on their faces lingered.

The alarm screeched at 5. ripping them away from their dreams. They shifted and locked in a kiss.

In fifteen minutes, she tapped a swift message to her crew, and by 5:30, she was up, dressing in a flurry. Clothes snapped into place pretty quickly.

"You're a storm," he blinked, marvelling.

"Boarding school habits," she informed, laughing at the same time.

They gulped down some more hot water.

He tugged on his shoes, wrapped her in a tight hug, pressed a kiss on the mole on her nose, and hoisted her bag onto his shoulders. At the gate, their farewell was a long, wordless gaze, love oozing out of every cell in their bodies.

She slipped into her car and drove off into the dawn while he rode away in his, the melody of 'isharo isharo main' playing in a loop in his thoughts.

•

Chapter 10

Meet the Siblings

RUDRA sat on his bed, reminiscing about the time he spent with Kavya, when his phone buzzed with the possibility of an urgent meeting at the party office. He wished he could take the day off, but duty had already begun to grasp him in its iron grip. The day seemed to be slipping away like sand through his fingers.

The phone rang again, its shrill cry slicing through the silence. He upswiped the green icon.

Gulnaaz spoke from the other side, her usual brightness snuffed out. “Rudra Sir, it’s bad. The truck protests are turning nasty. Clashes erupting everywhere, police swinging batons, protestors shoving back.”

His chest tightened at the news.

“How bad?” he questioned, his mind already sprinting in thought of the disaster.

"It's unravelling fast," she said, panic in her voice. "Blood has been spilt. It's a wildfire now."

Rudra shut his eyes. Flashes of the protest leaders' faces rent through his mind. He'd sat with them and listened to their grievances. They'd craved justice, but why then had they decided to give in to causing such carnage? Such a large-scale violence… it just didn't fit.

His stomach twisted into knots.

This wasn't the plan.

"There's more," Gulnaaz said. "I heard the rural artisans have formed a group, and they met with the government to lodge their protests on the new zoning policies and also to request to end the truck protests end. They're threatening a protest at Azad Maidan as well."

Artisans. Protest. How would this affect Kavya? He wondered.

Did she know? Had she spoken with the artisans?

"But the government officials have so far calmed down the artisans," Gulnaaz continued. "Or so I heard."

He breathed a sigh of relief. The artisans had backed down. For now. But for how long?

"Gulnaaz, I need it all. Every update, every detail, live as it happens. Watch those protests like a hawk."

He ended the call and dialled Satya, his social media lifeline. "Satya, dig in. Every post, every hashtag, every scream online about these protests. Gauge the heat, the spread, all of it." The sooner the transport protests come to an end, the better. It was affecting his spiritual tourism venture as well.

The phone slipped from his hand, thudding onto the mattress.

A sigh leaving his lips, he looked at the ceiling, its blank expanse mocking his helplessness. The protest had started small, but now it was becoming a maelstrom. And it had to come right at this time. The elections were only three months away.

"Damn protests!"

CocoArt Cafe was popular for the bittersweet tang of chocolate and the faint crackle of melting sugar. Rudra had picked the spot deliberately since this was the first official date with Kavya after he slipped the ring onto Kavya's finger. He was sure that she'd lose herself in this haven of indulgence. The very thought of it made him feel proud of his choice.

He sprawled across a velvet couch, its deep plum cushions sinking beneath him, and fixed his gaze on the glass doors. His fingers kept tapping on the table. He already forgot the protests happening in the state, though they pricked the edges of his mind like jagged thorns. He would not think about them. Not when Kavya's just about to walk in.

She swept in through the entrance like a gust of autumn, her dress rippling around her in waves of amber and moss green. Her hair tumbled free today, no bunstick in sight, spilling over her shoulders in a cascade of dark silk. She glowed, her presence making his heart beat faster. The shadows beneath her eyes told him she was tired, but the weariness didn't feature in her approach. She looked vibrant and beautiful.

She slid onto the couch across from him, her hand darting to grasp his. The touch felt as though a live wire had sparked beneath his skin. "Hey, Rudra," she greeted.

"Hey, Kavya," he murmured as he stared at her. Her sharp jaw. The dusting of freckles. The way her lips quirked, just so. "You look stunning."

She laughed, bubbling up, her cheeks red. "And you look…. well-rested," she shot back, her eyes teasing him with a glint.

He smirked. "Now that you're here, I'm finally at peace."

Silence nestled in between them. Their hands stayed locked. The cafe's chatter was just background noise they didn't bother about.

Rudra decided to break the silence first. "We need to talk… about our families."

Kavya's grip tightened. "Yeah, we do."

He breathed deep, the scent of chocolate and vanilla wafting into his nose. "I think we should tell our parents, but maybe… maybe we wait for Diwali. It's big, festive, and auspicious. Feels right for this."

Her brows furrowed. "Diwali? That's months away, Rudra. Why drag it out?"

He shifted in his seat. "I know it's not soon, but I want us to have this time. Just us. My dad's a little stuck in his ways. I need to ease him into it. And Diwali's perfect for our families to meet. Everyone's together. The vibe's good."

She gnawed at her lips. He could feel her wrestling with it. "Fine," she said at last, "but what if we tell our siblings first?"

Relief washed through him. "That's genius. We bring them in, get them on our side, and then hit the parents together. I'd feel steadier with that."

Her face softened. "Good, I'll tell Mihir then. He's around. I need him to know."

"I'd love to meet him," he said. "Whenever he's free, I'm there."

"You will? And what about your siblings? When can I meet them?"

"Soon," he promised. "Very soon."

Tension drifted away.

When the waiter came, they ordered some chocolate fondue and hot chocolate. Dripping strawberries and steaming mugs soon crowded the table. Rudra watched her spear a berry.

Earlier, his future had felt teetering. Now, with Kavya's laughter in his ears, it felt solid. Something he could hold on to.

When Rudra entered the party office later, he found it to be a hive of bustling activity. Posters, campaign slogans, and a myriad of maps plastered the walls in such a way that each item felt like a strategic puzzle piece in the larger political game. The protests, now turning violent, had become a major concern for the party, and as such, he had received a call asking him to come meet the campaign manager.

When Rudra entered the party office later that afternoon, he found posters, campaign slogans, and a myriad of maps plastered across the walls. Each such item felt like a strategic piece of a ginormous political puzzle. Once mere rumblings of discontent, the transport protests had erupted into violence. Tension coiled around the room like a living thing.

The campaign manager had summoned him here. Once he entered the former's cabin, the clamour in the entire office faded into something distant. A handful of framed certificates decorated the otherwise bare walls of the room. A desk lay at the far end, beside the window, so polished it gleamed under the overhead light. Books and files were aligned on the desk with a military-style precision.

The cabin's occupant was a man who was a veteran of many political battles. He had always admired him, seeing in him a mentor who thrived in the brutal game of power.

"Rudra, thank God you're here," the manager said. His sharp and unyielding eyes locked onto him. "This transport protest is spiralling out of control. We need it contained. Now."

His chest tightened. "I'm on it, Sir. What's the latest?"

The manager leaned forward. "Violence's escalating day by day. It ain't a protest anymore. Someone's stoking the fire, and I need to know who. If we don't choke this off now, it'll torch our campaign."

His mind churned. Why him?

He was the youngest in the ranks. A steady hand, but no master negotiator. Not like him. This felt bigger than the usual assignments. He tilted his head. "Sir, if I may… why me? There are others with more experience."

The manager's lips thinned. "You've built a rapport with them, Rudra. They might yet listen to you more than they would to anyone on our side. That trust is gold right now."

Fair enough, he thought.

Rudra nodded, freed of doubts. "I understand, Sir," he said. "I'll do whatever it takes."

"Good. Dig deeper. Find out who's inciting this mess. I suspect outside hands are stirring the pot, trying to smear us. Get me names."

"I'll find them, Sir," he said in a firm voice. "I've got a few threads to pull already. But I'll need a team. People who'll follow my lead without hesitation."

"You've got it. My full support… just tread carefully. This isn't only about politics anymore. It's about keeping people safe."

He dipped his head. "I'll handle it, Sir. You'll hear from me soon."

Turning back, he stepped back into the fray of the office. The chaotic din crashed over him like a wave. Volatile stakes lay ahead of him, but he'd see it through.

At half past noon the next day, Rudra slumped in his VP cabin, the old air-conditioner rattling like an old man's last gasp. Beads of sweat trickled down his neck, soaking his collar. He muttered a litany of curses at the useless machine.

The sun scorched through the window, taunting him with its relentless glare. He loathed the heat, but it was the waiting that gnawed at him. Minutes dragged into hours. Just as his patience frayed, his phone buzzed.

KK: Rudra, Mihir wants to meet you today.

Excited by the message, he banished his hatred for the heat from his mind. At first, they decided on a Chinese restaurant called Manchuria Kitchen, but after reading through a lot of reviews, and found Chimmichurri to have the perfect vibe for this meeting. Kavya didn't hesitate to agree. Soon after, she texted him again.

KK: Mihir's in for 2:30.

Rudra grinned.

He rolled into Chimmichurri's parking lot just as their car slid in beside his. Their tyres crunched gravel as they came to a stop.

"Rudra!" Kavya's voice cut through the traffic noise, pulling his head around.

His lips curled into a wide smile as he clasped Mihir's hand. A solid grip and a quick mutual scan.

Mihir looked younger than he had imagined. The former's shirt had been pressed sharply, his smile carrying the same warmth as Kavya.

Rudra's eyes then flicked to her, and his breath snagged. She stood there in a black top, hugged by an embroidered jacket. Her handiwork, he presumed. She radiated poise, and looking at her, something fierce stirred in his chest.

He longed to embrace her tightly, but he tamped it down, offering a handshake instead.

They entered the restaurant, rock music playing in the background with neither too high nor too low volume-wise. They chose a table near the back.

Rudra eased into his chair, levelling a look at the brother. "You drink?" He had hesitated at first, but he decided to test the waters.

Mihir nodded, unfazed.

"Chivas Regal, 12, 30 ml?" Rudra pressed.

Another nod.

He waved at the waiter and placed his and Mihir's orders.

"Gin, 30 ml, water, lime juice," Kavya ordered, carrying the tonal authority he had come to adore.

"And what about food, Ma'am, Sirs?" the water asked.

For food, she pitched sizzlers, her gaze flicking to both him and Mihir. He agreed. Mihir did as well.

Despite his meat-leaning options, they followed suit with vegetarian options with no fuss.

Kavya's idea is genius. He bends without breaking.

Mihir leaned in. "So, what exactly do you do?" he asked. His voice carried a probing edge Rudra had come to recognise so well. He wondered how much he could tell. Politics was a beast to unpack. Shadowy deals, long games, stakes that could sink a person. Rudra held the brother's stare and did not flinch.

"Five years in the thick of politics," he answered. "Core team for a senior politician. Started with a fellowship, cut my teeth on campaigns, now I'm VP of government affairs for a private outfit. Policy, advisory, and greasing the wheels with the government. That's my lane."

Mihir tilted his head as he processed.

Rudra, though, could sense the doubts. He was, however, not surprised.

"Why politics?" Mihir dug deeper. "You could serve people anywhere."

Rudra smiled. He'd been asked the same question before. "Power trumps cash for me. Politics scales service like nothing else, lets me do good and make it last. It's not just altruism. It's leverage."

Mihir twitched his lips. There was a grudging respect in his eyes that Rudra acknowledged.

Their talk veered into different topics, one of them being war and peace. Their viewpoints and ideas clashed like flint on steel.

"Violence can pave the way to peace," Rudra argued, tossing out history's bloodiest proofs.

Mihir countered with a dreamer's hope, to which he just tipped his head.

"If your path holds, fine. If it crumbles, I'd use whatever works."

As they finished their sizzlers and drained their glasses, Rudra suggested a smoke break, signalling the waiter for another round when they came back.

Mihir opened up about his work in the real estate sector. "I'm grinding for the CAT again," he said, laying his ambition bare. "Missed the IIMs last year, but I'll get it this time."

Rudra smiled, liking the fire in him. It matched Kavya's flame to flame.

Over whiskey and cigarettes, they traded laughs and barbs. The mood loosened until Mihir let slip their father's suspicions, apparently sparked by a driver's loose lips. "If we hadn't met today, he'd be on Kavya's case tonight," Mihir said, half-grinning.

Rudra felt his guts clench, but Kavya's steady look anchored him.

At 5 P.M., Mihir checked his watch. "Meeting's calling."

Kavya's eyes lingered on Rudra, pleading with him to stretch the moment a little longer. He felt the same pull, but Mihir's firm nudge won out. He warned us through his actions not to tempt fate.

They split up, Kavya driving off with her brother, while Rudra watched their taillights fade.

He yanked out his phone.

RR: Bro, I wanted more time with you.

Her reply came fast.

KK: I know, but we've got to play it smart.

He let out an exasperated sigh. She was right. They needed to be cautious.

For now.

Rudra slipped out the office's rear door, swallowed by the alley's shadows. The stench of stale cigarettes and damp concrete made him wrinkle his nose, but he persevered on through the alley until he reached a dark corner. His two contacts, Harish and Ravi, emerged near the back exit.

Harish was a burly frame of muscle, his arms tattooed all over. Beside him, Ravi stood wiry and restless. Smoke spiralled upward from their cigarettes, mixing with the alley's smell.

"Harishbhai, Ravibhai, I need you on this," he said. "The transport protests are boiling over. Someone's lit a fire. Find out who. Dig into their lives. Where they've been, who they run with, what drives them. I want the raw truth, not shadows."

Harish squinted. "What's the play, boss? You after their rap sheets, political strings?"

Rudra felt his gaze sharpen. "Everything. Their histories, their allies, their reasons for inciting this chaos. I need ammunition, not rumours."

Ravi's eyes glinted. "We've got people. We'll turn over every stone."

He nodded. "Keep it silent. No trails. Bring me proof. Names. Dates. Hard facts. Nothing less."

Harish nodded. "You've got it, Rudrabhai," he said, voice gravelly. "We'll bring you the bones."

They faded into the alley's darkness as Rudra watched. He turned towards the exit when a sudden creepiness crawled up his spine. He quickly scanned the alleyway and caught a fleeting shift behind a dumpster. A shadow darted, vanished in an instant. Someone was out there, spying on him. He promised he would find them out soon.

The next evening, Rudra found out that Kavya's father had come to Mumbai and stayed with her at her Airbnb. He couldn't meet Kavya tonight, as neither of them wanted her father to have questions about their relationship. Both of them had agreed they would keep their relationship secret and would only tell them when they both were ready. He had pressed for Diwali, but it did not look like Kavya would wait until then. Although he hoped she would. He took out his phone and started texting instead.

RR: Well, I've got an idea. Can you ask Mihir to take you on a drive tonight? And then I'll join you.

KK: I'll try.

Some time passed before her next text message arrived.

KK: Mihir agreed. Let's meet up at 10 and go for a drive.

RR: Good.

KK: Where should we pick you from, Rudra?

RR: Pick me from my home.

By 10 P.M., he was wired and paced the porch, adrenaline rushing through him. His ears pricked up at the sound of an approaching engine. He saw Mihir's car pull up fifteen minutes late. Although his heart twisted as he spotted Sanaya in the back seat.

Her again?

She reminded him of Kavya's old prank. The latter, now his girlfriend, had pushed him towards Sanaya over a shared quirk. What was it? Something about each of them having one organ less. He remembered that Sanaya had lost a gall bladder. The prank's sting flared for a brief moment, but watching Kavya climb out of the car stifled the feeling down.

Kavya smiled at him and asked him to climb into the car. As he did, she slid in beside him, while Sanaya shifted to the front.

He wanted to pull her closer towards him, but his parents' voice echoed in his ears. Not tonight, he convinced himself. Instead, he drank her in. Her blue linen pyjamas hung loose, a pink top caught the streetlight, spectacles rode low on her nose. There was no bunstick again today. Her hair roamed free, creating an outline around her face that made his breath whistle. Her eyes caught his, and Rudra felt his world shake.

Their hands found each other in the back seat as Mihir gunned it towards Sky Lounge. The shopfronts bled neon into the black, the air sharp with the smell of diesel and night-blooming jasmine. Her fingers laced through his, tight and sure, and Rudra held on as though she might vanish if he let her go.

Sky Lounge was a rooftop bar sprawled under a sky punched with stars. The Bollywood band played a lazy rhythm. The four of them split off. Mihir and Sanaya claimed a table by the railing while Rudra remained with Kavya closer to the band.

Beers hit the table with loud clinks, condensation beading cold against his palm. He grabbed a napkin, wrote isharo isharo main on it, and slipped it to the singer with a nod.

The tune rolled out, bringing them closer together.

Kavya laughed and then flagged the waiter. She ordered some green tea.

Their hands clasped each other tightly on the table, her thumb grazing his knuckles.

His eyes went to her hair and wondered why she had not worn her bunstick. Had she lost hers? Or was it a sign?

Should he gift her a bunstick? After all, at a point in time, he had decided he would gift her a golden bunstick. He made a note in his mind to arrange for it once he got back to the house.

Midnight crept up. How time had passed so quickly!

They left the lounge and stepped onto the street.

He led them to an ice-cream parlour he knew.

It was a dim nook with a flickering sign.

Kavya grasped raspberry sticks for herself and Mihir. Sanaya took mango. Rudra, on the other hand, ever the outlier, picked Gulaab e Jannat. When he told them, it elicited a round of laughter. They passed the cone around, the floral sweetness melting on their tongues. For the moment, the four of them clicked. Rudra wanted the time to freeze right then.

Half past midnight, Kavya's phone lit up. Her father's stern voice cackled through.

And then reality crawled back in.

They piled into the car, and Mihir drove them homeward. Outside his gate, he stepped out. Kavya did too.

They exchanged a hug.

And then she sat back in the car.

Mihir stepped on the pedal and drove away. Rudra stood there, watching the car disappear.

A few minutes later, he took out his phone and started to type.

RR: Bro, I wanted to spend time with you alone.

KK: I know, but we've got to be careful. Dad is always asking questions, always suspicious.

He cursed and put his phone back in his pocket.

Letting out a deep sigh, he promised himself that he would wait. And one day, there would be no restrictions.

Chapter 11

My Sister is my Mentor!

A couple of days later, Rudra couldn't stop glancing at the clock. Kavya's trip to Mumbai was locked in for 4 P.M. Mihir was going to bring her here. She had a shoot to attend first, and then they were supposed to be at their relatives' place for Rakshabandhan the next evening.

The festival had passed a few days ago. Even though she had been with her brother that night, they had decided to have their Rakshabandhan at the same time as their cousins were having theirs. He, on the other hand, had been busy, unable to return to Nashik, though his hometown and sister's memories tugged at him. He had planned to go to Nashik on the eve of tomorrow. Obligations lingered in his mind like a late monsoon rain.

Her family was supposed to arrive in the afternoon, so she would only have a day to spend with him. None of them was about to let it slip through their fingers. They had decided to have dinner at a posh restaurant in Mulund, and he couldn't wait for it.

Mihir, he learned, would be crashing at a friend's place and dropping her off at 9:30 P.M.

Rudra, though, hit a snag. Work flared up out of nowhere. There was a sudden blaze of emails and calls that kept him tethered to his phone. This ended up with him being late by half an hour, palms sweaty, tie loosened.

Kavya had soup and pizza waiting, her eyes surveying his entire self as though trying to decode the kind of stress he was in. Between his distracted spoonfuls, her fingers grazed his. She whispered, I love you, a sentence that cut through his skull.

He slurped the broth and nudged the pizza aside, though he requested the waiter to parcel it up. After having dinner, Rudra drove his car through traffic to his place and arrived at fifteen past eleven. No matter the time, though, cars still choked the roads. Entering the apartment, Rudra saw her notice the house. His roommate, Jignesh, had his fingerprints mark every inch of the apartment. Vintage chairs swathed in embroidered throws. Lamps spilt pools of ambient light. Walls felt alive with art that screamed tradition. It hit Rudra every time. This space was not a crash pad. It was like a second skin.

"Rudra, this doesn't scream bachelor at all!" Kavya's laugh rang out, her eyes wide as she spun in place.

He grinned. "Blame my roommate, Jignesh. I'm just squatting in his masterpiece."

"I need to meet this guy," she said, curious.

"Next time you're here," he promised.

They dropped onto the sofa, tugged the balcony curtains shut, and let the room shrink around them. Her lips found his, soft in the beginning, sharp after. Their breaths tangled and bodies tilted together until no gap remained. He felt his blood roar in his ears.

"Bedroom?" Kavya's whisper grazed his ear.

He answered with a kiss.

Harder. Hungrier.

His hands traced the curve of her spine.

Together, they stumbled thus down the hall, laughter tripping over their desire, shedding clothes for worn tees and shorts. Rudra scrubbed toothpaste across his teeth in a haze. When he asked her, she smirked at him. "Too lazy!" she moaned.

Under the sheets, her head tucked against his chest, his arm slung over her like a barricade. Their breathing synced, and then the night swallowed them whole.

At half past six in the morning, Rudra awoke, sunlight slipping in through the blinds. He rolled closer, nuzzling her neck with sweet, sleepy kisses, her skin warm against his lips. Her grip tightened on his hand; he dozed off again. The next three hours were just spent in half-dreams.

When they woke up, he found her looking around. "Rudra, I drink a litre of water a day, and you've only got 700 ml here," she teased.

He hauled himself up, grabbed another bottle from the kitchen, and tossed it her way with a lopsided grin. She had this pull, dragging him into her workaholic world, making him want to step up. By ten in the morning, they pried themselves from the bed. He needed to buy gifts for his sister. They wouldn't buy themselves.

Kavya shoved him towards the bathroom, brushing alongside him, toothpaste flecks on her chin as she kept them on track.

Very soon, he found himself tagging along with her in a popular mall. He didn't know what to get his sister, but fortunately for him, Kavya had come with him. She zeroed in on a bag she swore his sister would adore.

Ayushi, another one of her friends, swept in. Quick-witted and warm as she was, Rudra felt another layer of Kavya click into place. Ayushi herded them to Trends for slippers. Soon, they snagged a pair each before bolting to her store. Kavya's parents were due at her store by half past two. Mihir, though, beat them there and leaned on his car with a lazy grin.

For lunch, they went to a place called Rekdi Club, a vegan joint that had Rudra and Mihir swap wary glances. Tofu pretending to be meat didn't sell them, but they forked through it, wanting to keep Kavya happy.

"So what'd you two do last night?" Mihir asked casually.

Rudra's fork hovered in the air for a brief moment. "Dinner. Crashed after," he snickered. "Beats this vegan mastery, though."

Mihir barked a laugh and then changed the topic to stock markets. Numbers flew until Rudra checked his watch. 2:30

was closing in. "I have to head to Nashik now," he said, the words tasting sour.

Kavya nodded and hugged him.

Kissing her an 'I Love You,' he exited the restaurant, picking a rose pastry on the way out. As he sat in his car, he typed:

RR: I wanted more time.

KK: Me too.

If he could, he would have clawed for more time. Right now, though, Rashmi beckoned.

The sprawling, two-story house in Nashik was a welcome sight for Rudra. As he drove up the tree-lined driveway, the scent of blooming jasmine filled the air, the familiar aroma a comforting reminder of home. He had reached Nashik around 6 PM, the setting sun casting a warm, golden glow over the property, and a sense of peace settled over him, a welcome change from his hectic routine. He was always happy when he was with his family, and he had been looking forward to spending some quality time with them, especially his sister, whom he hadn't seen in months.

Rudra's car crunched gravel underneath its tyres as he rolled up the driveway to the two-story house in Nashik. It rose up in front of him like an old friend against the softening night sky. The scent of blooming jasmine filled the air, its sweet tang weaving through the dusk, tugging him back to the summers spent chasing Rashmi across the lawn. This house was a gift from his parents for Rashmi, given during the wedding, so that they could stay in the same city. His brother-in-law owned a successful IT startup here, while his sister had her own entrepreneurial venture. She did come to Mumbai sometimes. They'd meet whenever they both were free. But these meetings were rare. He looked forward to meeting her today after a long time. He was already feeling guilty for not having made it on the day of the festival itself.

He'd hit his destination by six in the evening, a relatively fast ride. The weather was cooler here, most welcome after Mumbai's relentless churn.

He swung the car door shut and strode towards the porch. Laughter echoed in the living room, a bright, unruly sound that made him grin before he had even crossed the threshold. Rashmi spotted him first, her dark hair knotted in a sloppy bun. Her kurta seemed stitched by threads that danced in the lamplight. She barreled over and slammed into him with a hug that squeezed the breath from his lungs. The months apart from her melted with a single touch.

He smiled. She was still his rock, the one who could read him like an open book. His mind, though, reminded him that there was now one other person who could share that title.

Kavya.

"Rudra!" She crowed, pulling back to muss his hair. "I was starting to think you'd forgotten where my home is."

He swatted her hand away, smirking. "Missed you, too, trouble. It's been too long since I've had to dodge your bad ideas."

She squinted at him, hands on her hips, sizing him up like a hawk would its prey. "Hold up… you're glowing, Bhai… What's the deal? New haircut? Or… wait… don't tell me… You've got a girlfriend?"

Heat crept up his neck. Regardless, he met her stare. "She's not just any girl, Rashmi. She's the charm pulling me through."

Her jaw dropped and then snapped shut as she yanked him inside and plopped him onto the living room sofa. "Spill it! Who's got you all mushy? I need details. Name. Face. The works!"

Rudra laughed. Keeping Kavya under wraps had never been an option when he had come here. Rashmi had a nose for secrets.

He leaned back, letting the cushions swallow him. He started at the beginning. Their first date. Their meetings are after. Kavya's work with the artisans. Her quick wit. "She's got this edge, you know? Fierce but kind. Drags me out of my own head."

Rashmi propped her chin on her hand, eyes wide and gleaming. "And the proposal? I want the full scene, okay?"

"A restaurant, late night, pizza on the table," he said. "I just told her… No big plan… just her, me, and the truth."

She smacked his arm and snorted an "Ugh!"

"You're so smitten!" she said. "But she sounds like a keeper. When do I get to meet her, though?"

"Soon," he promised, dodging another swat. "You'll love her. She's got your kind of spark… well, minus the hair-ruffling obsession."

Their chatter stopped as Dhawal, his brother-in-law, walked in.

Rudra had always liked the guy. He was steady as a rock, sharp in his IT hustle, the kind of man you could lean on.

"Rudra, man, you're alive!" Dhawal clapped his shoulder. "What kept you away so long?"

"Work's a beast," he said. "Here for a night. Back to the grind tomorrow."

"Then we're milking it," Dhawal shot back. "Rakhi's still on, late or not. You're stuck with us."

His gaze flickered to a smirking Rashmi. He let out a sigh. "Actually, I came here to flaunt my girlfriend, but it seems Rashmi's already sniffed her out."

Dhawal's brows shot up. "Oh yeah? Who's gotten you all committed and smitten?"

Rudra dove back into his story, sketching Kavya's world. Dhawal nodded along, placing a steady hand on his shoulders.

The night carried on with Rakhi rituals. Rashmi's thread wound tight around his wrist, her teasing grin widening as he handed over the gift he had purchased at the mall. A gift Kavya had chosen.

His sister then piled food on the plates. As they ate, they swapped stories about work and oddball hobbies. Rudra let slip bits about his tech PR gig, the small dents he'd made in this world. Here, he didn't have to prove a damn thing.

"She's a find, Rudra!" Dhawal said later, sprawled across an armchair. "You've landed a good one."

His chest swelled. "Yeah, she's the real deal. You'll see."

In bed that night, Rudra replayed the events of the evening in his mind. Rashmi's ribbing. Dhawal's nod. The way Kavya's shadow loomed even here. Peace settled in his mind. He'd bared his soul to the people who mattered to him the most. And they'd caught it without a flinch.

There was literally no noise outside on the streets of Nashik, but Rudra's room buzzed with Kavya's voice. She spoke low on the other side of the phone. Rudra knew that she was being cautious enough not to speak loudly. He could hear the murmurs of her family in the background. He could picture her in his mind, huddled in some corner, her breath hitching as she dodged her father's ears. Their secrecy created distance between them, making him hate it.

Morning came early, and with it came her call. Rudra pressed his phone closer to his ears to ensure he actually heard her low voice. By the time the clock read 10 A.M., she had already contacted him twice. This was the third time she had called. This time, though, her voice splintered. A sob slipped out, making him almost clench his fists. It hurt him that she cried. "Kavya, what's wrong?" he asked, his tone steady. "I'm here; don't cry; tell me."

She called Rudra early the next morning, her voice soft, full of precaution. It was like being back in school, communicating in secret, constantly wary of being caught.

"My family's out there… in the drawing room," she stuttered. "Dad brought up the marriage topic… questioning why I'm not getting hitched… and I just hate it. Felt like a spotlight I couldn't dodge. Snuck off to my room."

He exhaled. "Hey, it's alright, Kavya. Our folks… they fuss because they care. Doesn't mean they've got us all figured out."

Her crying eased a bit, but the ache lingered in his chest. After a time of quiet murmurs, her breathing steadied on the other end of the line. They ended the call, but he couldn't stop talking to her. He fired off a text.

RR: I love you. No tears, okay?

KK: Rudra, crying to you felt safe. Thanks for being you.

RR: Always on your team, no matter what.

After an hour had passed, he dialled her again to check on her. This time, she answered more brightly.

"Stuffed myself silly, feeling better now," she said.

Rudra grinned, relieved.

"Good, take care of yourself," he said, ending the call again.

After the terse conversation, he made himself sprawl across the faded sofa in his sister's living room. The scent of roasted cumin from her kitchen wafted into his nose, bringing back memories of his childhood. He remembered the time when he and his sister used to swipe late-night snacks from the kitchen without their parents knowing.

Rashmi flopped beside him, her kurta bunched at her knees, and picked a peanut from the bowl between them and flicked it at his forehead. It bounced off with a dull thwack.

"Oi, genius," she said, grinning, "you've got that goofy look again. Still mooning over Kavya, huh?"

He swatted at the air, picking a peanut to launch at his sister. "Shut it, trouble. She's not some crush I'm doodling about. She's the real deal."

Rashmi dodged his peanut attack and laughed. "Oh, I believe it, lover boy. You're practically glowing; it makes me wanna puke." She leaned towards him with her eyes narrowed. "But you're fidgeting worse than when you broke Dad's old radio. What's eating you?"

His grin faltered.

Rashmi always saw through him. She was his mentor, his sister, a pain in the ass. All rolled into one. "Alright, fine!" he muttered. "Should I tell Mom and Dad? About her, I mean. Feels like I'm hiding a damn novel under my bed."

Her smirk softened. "You're asking me? The one who coached you through sneaking out of the house at sixteen?" She snatched the peanut bowl and popped one of them into her mouth. "Tell them, you dolt. Truth's the only way with those two. They'll sniff out a lie faster than I can steal your fries."

He groaned. "Easy for you to say. You're the golden kid. What if they flip? Dad's still stuck on his proper timeline nonsense."

Rashmi jabbed his arm. "Please," she snorted, "I've got my own dents in that golden crown. Look, Rudra, they might grumble, sure. But they love you. Kavya's gold, from what you tell me. But they'll see it once you stop skulking around like a thief. You're not sixteen anymore. So quit acting like it."

He nodded. She'd always been his compass.

"So, just… rip the bandage off?"

"Yep," she said, flicking another peanut at him. "And when they meet her, I'll be there to gush so they can't fuss. Now quit moping, dolt. Grab me a soda. You owe me for the wisdom."

Rudra laughed. "Bossy as ever!" he shot back.

She was right. He ought to tell his parents, but he still wanted to stick to his Diwali timeline. He believed that was the auspicious time. He now knew that his sister would be with him when he told his parents.

He peeled out of his sister's home at half past five and reached his home at seven. Kavya and her kin had already left Mumbai at 7 and were slated to reach their home at 11. He shot her a text.

RR: Convince Mihir for a drive tonight?

KK: Tried. He's out. Says we've gotta cool it. Or Dad'll catch on!

When she got home, her call came fast.

"Rudra, can you get to my terrace? It's dead up there. Nobody ever checks. Lift to the seventh, straight across, there's this little nook off the main stretch. Safe."

He felt his pulse quicken, wanting to meet her. But the reality posed a risk to the venture. "Kavya, listen," he said, keeping his tone even. "That's a huge gamble. The lift buzzes. Steps echo. Anyone's bound to notice. We're not in a film reel here."

She huffed. "But it'd be perfect.... like those stories we love."

"You're already my wild plot twist," he chuckled. "Don't need a chase scene to prove it."

Her sigh cackled through, but she relented. "Fine, you win. Tomorrow then? Early lunch?"

"Judo's Bar and Cafe?" he suggested. "Noon sharp."

The talk veered then to old romantic gestures. They traded favourites and talked along as the night deepened. After hours passed, the clock running past midnight, sleep pressed in. "In a while, crocodile," he muttered his signature farewell.

"See you later, alligator," came her faint signature response from the other side.

As the echo settled, Rudra fell asleep, sinking into his dreams of her.

Rudra woke with Kavya's voice still playing in his ears. All night, he'd replayed spending time with her in a loop, thinking of different ways to gift her the golden bunstick he'd placed an order for. He had researched two companies and ordered one from each. Whichever was the best one, I'd gift her. Both companies had promised me delivery within seven to eight business days.

He shrugged into a shirt when a restless itch took hold. He wanted to see her in something traditional today. So, he shot off a text.

RR: Wear something Indian. Let's see what you got.

She pinged back fast.

KK: Done, your Highness!

He smirked as he imagined her raised brows.

By one in the afternoon, he reached Judo's Bar and Cafe. This place buzzed quite softly compared to the other places they had been to together. Spoons clicked against mugs. The espresso machine snarled. A whiff of toasted bread and cardamom spiked the air. He sat at a table by the window and waited, fidgeting impatiently all along. Some time passed before the door chimed. He turned to see Kavya sweep towards him. The sight of her made him fall into a trance-like state. Her brown and gold kurta clung sharply to her skin. Pyjama swished at her ankles. Her dupatta slung loose like a dare. She seemed taller in it, a queen in motion. The mascara smudged around her eyes like midnight pools. The silver stick in her bun flashed under the ambient lights, but it was the mole on her nose that hooked him.

Every time.

She lunged at him, arms coiling tight. He pressed his chin into her hair, inhaling her rose scent. Then she sprang up, and her lips touched his. A quick, impish peck.

"Kavya, you'll kill me in public one day," he laughed.

She dropped into her seat. "Good. Keeps you sharp."

Their hands locked across the table. He flagged a waiter and ordered a honey ginger lemon, which was her mountain elixir, and he wished for himself a bun maska with extra butter oozing hot across the plate. He also added masala chai to the order so as to chase it down his throat. They split the bun, tearing it with their greasy fingers.

"I'm telling Dad about us soon."

He felt his gut lurch. "What if we wait? Diwali's close. Give him a softer landing."

She shook her head. "No can do, Rudra. Can't hide any longer. My father's already circling around my secrets. I'd rather swing first."

He frowned. "Just… watch your step, okay? I don't want them turning on you."

She smiled. "Stop worrying; I'll handle it." She clapped. "It's going to work!"

He let out a breath. "If you're sure, I'm in."

Her face ignited, leaning close. "Oh, thank you!"

"Want to meet my sister?" he asked.

She blinked, caught off guard. "Wait, now?"

"Yes, Rashmi's office is across the street. She could be here in twenty."

Kavya widened her eyes. She looked like a kid on a sugar rush. "Yes! Get her here!"

He took out his phone, racing his thumbs over the screen.

RR: Hey, want to meet my girlfriend?

Rashmi: You're joking, right?

RR: No trouble!

Rashmi: Fine. Where? When?

He typed out the cafe's name and time.

Rashmi: Coming. 30 mins.

RR: Hurry up, sis. Make it 20, though.

He slid the phone away, grinning. He took a glance at Kavya and saw his future in her. Soon, he would have the girl he had always dreamed of having.

Rudra leaned back in his chair at the cafe, masala chai cooling in his cup, waiting for his sister to show up. She was usually punctual, but today was different. She must be caught up in work, he thought, and wondered whether Kavya would be able to meet Rashmi today. Just when he thought his sister might not come, Rashmi walked in through the open archway, her saffron and teal dupatta swirling behind her, her eyes glinting at him with a spark he'd known since his childhood. He'd barely blinked before Kavya took off on her feet, having barely completed her talk in different ways she could tell her father, the grin on her face hitting him square on his chest. Rashmi matched her. Two of his loved ones collided, the air around him feeling like the centre of a hurricane.

They ordered a masala chai and talked, their conversation flowing effortlessly from one topic to another. The way they conversed with each other, anyone would think they had known each other for years. They ordered another round of chai and dove into chatter that flowed as smoothly as ink on paper. The conversation changed from art to dreams without interruptions. He watched and listened, not once trying to butt into their talk. Rashmi's hands danced as she moved her lips incessantly, weaving tales of ditching a desk job for her design brand. Kavya leaned closer, eyes wide, soaking it up. They laughed together, the sound of it echoing across the brick walls, mingling with the clatter of cups and the low hum of a ceiling fan. If anyone saw them right now, they'd think the two were as thick as thieves for years, not minutes.

He sipped his chai, the spice biting his tongue, and caught the thread tying his loved ones. Art, raw and unfiltered. His gaze caught sight of the camaraderie growing between them, and he could not help but feel happy about it.

They were rolling now.

Rashmi was soon becoming an inspiration for Kavya, he noticed.

He felt sidelined, but that didn't matter a bit. Not really.

Seeing Kavya so lit up made his chest ache in a good way.

"It's been a slog, Kavya," Rashmi said, "but worth every bruise. You're on that road too, I can tell. Takes guts."

Kavya nodded. "You've got no idea how much that means. I want that strength. Yours. Juggling dreams and family. It's wild."

Rudra shifted in his seat, knowing full well their talk would veer to him now.

His sister smirked, tossing him a look. "This guy? Never settles. Always chasing better. Drives me up the wall he does. But it's why he's Rudra."

"He's incredible."

His sister laughed. "Yeah, and damn lucky too, if you ask me. Don't let him slip, Kavya. Little brothers get spoiled rotten around here. I swear he nabbed all the extra love growing up."

He flicked a napkin at her. "Lies," he snorted. "You hogged the spotlight. I just got the leftovers."

Kavya giggled.

He caught her glance. Private. Knowing. He sank into it.

The clock struck half past three. Kavya's watch glinted as she checked it. A shadow crossed her face just then. "Gotta run. Dad's got some inputs on the store." She tapped her phone, trying to book a cab, but Rashmi stopped her. "I'll drop you… My place is closer… five minutes from yours."

Kavya hesitated at first and then nodded. "Can't say no to that."

As they stood, Rashmi slung her arm around Kavya's shoulder and laughed as they trailed out the door. Rudra stayed behind to pay off the bill, watching them vanish into the afternoon glare. After clearing the bill, he hollowed out and took a solo walk homeward, quieter than he'd expected.

Chapter 12

Her Dad's Rejection

THE air in his home hit him with a slap of sizzling ghee and popping cumin. His mother's kitchen, no doubt, conjured the ghosts of his childhood. He stepped into the living room, lamps illuminating the threadbare rug, and sat on the sofa. With a deep breath, he clocked his father sitting on an ancient leather armchair, creased and story-scarred, a paperback horror dangling from his hands. The old man's eyes stared at him, sharp and curious, like he was the next plot twist.

His father stared back at him as well, curiosity in his eyes, his hands featuring a book. An avid reader that he was, his father always read books before he slept, and tonight, he was reading a popular horror one, apparently meant for kids. But then… When did his father ever mind about who the book's target audience was? His mother hovered at the sofa's edge, her fingers brushing his arm. Her touch made him want to cuddle up to his mother, but Rashmi's words weighed on his mind.

Tell them tonight, not tomorrow.

Could he tell them? About his love… the whole messy truth?

"Beta," his mother called out to him, her tone calming, "how was your day? Met Rashmi?"

Rudra felt his gaze dart to his father, who kept staring at him, the book now flat on his lap. He sucked in a lungful of air.

They'll get it. Rashmi had said.

He scraped up courage like coins from a pocket. "Yeah, I missed this place," he said, a half-smile making his lips curl halfway. "Rashmi's got stories for days."

His father leaned forward, the chair groaning under him. "And what else? Anything worth a tale?" He was blunt. It was his way, always looking for meat. Rudra had dodged many of the conversations like this since he was a kid sneaking candy past curfew. But there was going to be no dodging now. He straightened, meeting his eyes. He then turned to his mother. She was the softer target.

"Actually… there's something," he started, voice stuttering, "there's something I've been meaning to tell you both."

"Go on," his father said, sliding his book aside.

Rudra swallowed. "I've met someone. Her name's Kavya. She's incredible."

His mother's eyes flared wide. She grinned at him. "Rudra beta… Are you in love?" she asked in such an eager tone one would think she had been waiting for years to hear it.

He nodded, feeling the heat creep up his neck. "Yeah, Mom, I am. She's different. Lights me up in ways I didn't know I could feel."

His father cleared his throat, sounding gravelly. "Kavya, huh? What does she do?"

Rudra steadied himself. "She runs a business. Traditional crafts. Indian designs. She's all about her people. Her roots. She's sharp and intelligent. Honest too. Got this drive that…" He trailed off, imagining her in his mind. "She's got struggles, I don't lie, but she'll overcome."

The room stilled. His parents swapped glances with each other.

"Different, you say," his father grunted. "Never heard you talk like that about anyone. Must be something."

"She is, Dad," Rudra said firmly. "She gets me. My work. The politics. All of it. You'll love her, I know it."

His mother's hand found his cheek. "Oh, Rudra, we're so happy for you. She sounds like a gem. High time someone caught you."

His chest unclenched. Relief flooded through him. "Soon," he assured them. "But I want to do it right. Talk to her family first. Maybe after Diwali, when the dust settles."

His father's brow arched. "How long is that going to take?"

"After the festivals," Rudra said. "Gives us time to breathe. Set it up properly."

His parents traded another look. His mother's nod, though, sealed it.

"Alright, beta," she said. "We'll wait. But tell us more. She's got you glowing, and you've kept it hush for too long. You did well."

Rudra laughed.

The night spun on with him, sharing stories of Kavya with his parents. He'd take it slow, he would, but he wondered if Kavya would.

She had felt walls of secrets closing in on her, and she might not wait for Diwali.

He hoped she would, but doubt gnawed at his mind right then.

He received a text right then that confirmed his suspicion.

KK: I'm going to tell my father today.

Rudra knew that the day had finally arrived, the day Kavya was going to tell her father about their relationship. He had been certain in his mind that they would spend their lives together, their connection as strong as ever, their love a powerful force that had shaped their lives. They had met each other's siblings, had all bonded well, and things felt simpler, their love a guiding force through all their challenges. He also knew that his meeting with her father was not too far away, and a wave of nervousness, a sense of trepidation, washed over him.

He had always believed that Diwali was an auspicious occasion, a time of joy and celebration, but he wondered if they were tempting fate by pushing things forward before then. The thought of how Kavya would be handling the situation filled him with a mix of anxiety and apprehension. He wanted to do what was best for her, and he wanted everything to be perfect, but his control over the situation was limited.

His phone rang, the caller ID displaying Kavya's name, his heart pounding as he answered, the clock on the wall flashing 8:30 PM, a reminder of the long wait.

"Rudra, I'm going to tell my dad about us today or tomorrow," she said, her voice soft but laced with a mixture of anticipation and nervousness.

He immediately felt a sense of urgency, a wave of protectiveness washing over him. "Wait, Kavya," he said, his voice a little strained. "Think again. We could wait until Diwali and then take this further with a proper plan. We are already waiting so long, so what's a little more time?" He had always believed that patience was key, and he wanted them to take things slow.

"Rudra, Mihir and I decided that we'll take this further today. Rudra, I don't like seeing doubts in my father's mind. I want to clear and confess things with him. Everything will be fine, Rudra!" Her voice, though gentle, was filled with a conviction that he had always found both endearing and irresistible.

He felt a knot of anxiety tightening in his stomach. "I don't think so, Kavya. You should at least give me a chance to make things better. If you let me speak to him, then things will be fine."

"I'm sure Dad will be happy to know about us. Don't worry, I love you," she replied, her words a comfort to his troubled soul, a balm to his weary heart.

"I love you more," he said, his voice barely a whisper, his heart aching with a love that knew no bounds.

She disconnected the call, the sudden silence amplifying his anxiety, leaving him alone with his restless thoughts, his fears, and his uncertainty.

Kavya listened to the chime of the grandfather clock in the living room. It had become familiar like the sound of her heartbeat, though it did little to calm her anxiety. Outside the window, birds trilled their careless songs, flitting through the dusk. She remained perched on her chair's edge, fingers digging into the armrest, her breathing shallow and ragged. Her heart pounded against her ribs, every nerve in an overexcited drive. Today, she'd tell her father about Rudra. No more stalling. No more waiting for Diwali like Rudra wanted. Tradition and auspiciousness be damned, she couldn't wait any longer. Her father's affinity for digging out secrets wove walls around her, walls she could not break if they ever solidified.

She had made up her mind. Today was the day she would tell her father about Rudra. She'd cooked his favourites today. A simmering thick dal makhani, crisping gold parathas, hoping they would soften the blow. Her ears pricked up, catching the sound of crunched gravel outside. Tires rolled slowly on muddy tracks.

Jolting upright, she smoothed her kurta with shaky hands.

The door groaned open, her father stepping in. He wore a white kurta as a top and a dhoti as a bottom; the latter swaying as he took strides inside. His broad shoulders and unyielding gaze heightened his aura, something she'd been scared of since her childhood. She searched his face for any sign of negative emotions, praying his day hadn't soured him.

"Good evening, Baba," she greeted him.

He nodded with narrowing eyes. Did he see her fraying? She hoped not.

"Evening, Kavya," he rumbled, deep and even, and settled on the sofa with a sigh. "You're back early."

"Work was light today," she managed, polite as ever.

He harrumphed. "Mihir told me about the shoot as well. How did it go?"

"It went well, Baba, thank you." She forced a smile.

He tipped his head slowly. "Good, good, but still you look off today. Something up?"

She felt her chest tighten.

No more dodging, she told herself. She straightened, fingers brushing her dupatta's embroidery for a scrap of calm. "Actually, Baba, I've got something to tell you." She steadied herself. "I've been seeing someone. His name's Rudra. And I… I love him."

Silence stilled the room. Even the clock's familiar ticks seemed distant.

Her father's eyes darted to the floor, his face like a blank slate. She felt her stomach clench. He'd never gone this still before.

"Oh," he said at last, tone flat but edged, reeking of tension. "Rudra, huh? What's he doing?"

"He's in politics, Baba," she started, bracing for the storm. "But he's honest… amazing… driven."

His brows pinched. Eyes narrowed like blades. "Politics?" She knew he disliked the field. "A politician?"

She felt her gut sink. His tone felt like a shovel digging at her hope. "Not like that, Baba," she pushed back. "He's different, cares about people. Not just power. He's doing good."

"Politics is a cesspit, Kavya," he retorted. "It is full of unstable and crooked people. I didn't raise you to grow close to people like that."

"He's more than a politician. He runs a tech PR firm and a spiritual tourism gig, both solid. He's also VP of Governance for an MNC. Works with the government, not against it."

His lips twisted. "And just by telling it, you prove my words true. Entreat with the government? Smells like favours to me. Power games dressed up pretty. How's that honest?"

"No, Baba," she snapped. "He's not currying anything. He's real. He cares about his community. About me. I've met his sister too, and she's warm and genuine. You'd like her."

He stilled again. "I'll look into him," he said finally in a stony voice. "Need to know he's right for you. I won't settle for less."

Her shoulders sagged.

She got it. She was his shield. She was his love. But dread gnawed at her deep. "I know, Baba," she murmured. "Just give him a chance. He's not what you think. He makes me happy."

His gaze softened just then, love peeking through all that steel. "I'll try, beti, but I've got to be sure… for you."

She nodded. She needed his trust and his blessing. It wouldn't do her any good if she tried to argue about it further. "I love you, Baba," she whispered.

"Love you too," he said.

Silence stretched again.

And Kavya sank back, the clock's ticks clawing back in.

The whole thing would be a slog. Proving Rudra's worth. Chipping at her father's doubts. But she'd fight. Rudra was her truth, and she didn't plan to let him go that easily.

A day had passed since Kavya had decided to tell her father, and yet there was no response from her side. Rudra paced around his room, his mind racing, his thoughts colliding, his fears growing stronger; their love was his only solace. He wondered about their future, their responsibilities, and the lives they were building together. It was as though everything was finally coming together, and he wanted to ensure that he was ready for what was to come. He felt like he had finally grown up, that he was ready to take the next step, and he was willing to do whatever it took to spend his life with her. Rudra paced about his room, his boots scuffing the hardwood floor. A day had passed since Kavya had decided to tell her father, but there had been no response from her side. Her silence made him wonder about their future, their responsibilities, and the lives they were building together. He felt like he'd grown up overnight, ready to have a life with her.

Yanking out his phone, he thumbed over the keys, impatience flooding him. The clock read 9:30 P.M.

RR: Did you tell him?

KK: Yes.

RR: Is everything okay?

KK: Will call you in 15 mins.

Fifteen minutes stretched like a rubber band. Anxiety clasped his nerves with every tick of the clock.

RR: Please… tell me… At least if things are okay…

KK: Rudra, wait, I will call you in a few.

Her answer had come in anger. Anger, perhaps, at his impatience.

Why did she not understand? He had been patient throughout the day. Now, he could not wait for much longer. He needed to know what had transpired when she told her father about them. Something about it screamed that he might not have accepted their being together. He dialled her number, but she cut it dead. He swore under his breath and paced harder. His bare feet slapped the floor harder. Five minutes later, his phone lit up. "Rudra," she whispered. "Dad's got doubts. He doesn't get how you work for a politician and pull VP pay from a drone company. He thinks you're trading favours. Unethical, he said."

A sigh scraped his throat. Her father's suspicions weren't new. Dodging them was not an option. "Why didn't you tell them I'm an advisor or a consultant?" he asked.

"He's got questions, Rudra. Mihir and I tried. I told him about your family, your sister. Mihir vouched you're solid. But he's digging tomorrow. Be ready."

"I'll face it," he said, voice steely. "I'll meet him if he wants. Lay it all out for him."

"Wait," she cut in. "I'm gutted. He blindsided me with this."

"Kavya," he started, but she pushed on, giving voice to her father's thoughts and lectures on ethics. "I'm drained," she muttered. "Need sleep."

He bristled.

Sleep was her escape route. His, not so much.

"We can fix this now," he pressed. "I don't want to just sit here."

"I can't think straight right now, Rudra," she said. "I am done now."

She hung up.

He slammed the phone down. Its crack echoed across the hall.

It was their first fight. Their first fracture. And he hated it.

Sleep dodged him that night. Her words had hurt him. In the morning, guilt gnawed at him.

He dialled her again.

She answered fast. "Kavya, I'm sorry," he rasped. "Didn't mean to bulldoze you. Hated fighting."

"Rudra, I'm sorry, too," she murmured. "Ran from it... I shouldn't have."

"I couldn't sleep," he confessed. "It felt quite so wrong with you."

"Same," she agreed. "I needed you."

They talked for hours about what they should do. She suggested that they lean on her grandmother, but that was the last choice.

"We're good again," he said and ended the call.

Throughout the day, he carried on with calls and texts.

Work dragged him too. The protests had become intense, and there was no news from his two friends yet. He hauled home by night and received a text at half past nine.

KK: I'm with Dad.

He stared at it, feeling uncertain, wondering what her father was digging into now. Trusting her, he decided to wait, but the not-knowing carved a hole he could not easily fill.

Kavya felt the silence in the living room descend on her like a dreaded beast. All other sounds—the soft hum of the ceiling fan, the distant clatter of dishes from the kitchen, the occasional trill of a bird outside—were drowned in this sea of dread.

Kavya did not like the silence in the living room. It felt as if a dreaded beast had managed to land in the house and sucked in all the happiness. The ceiling fan whirred faintly overhead, dishes clinked somewhere down the hall, and a bird's trill spilt in through the open windows. Her heart pounded hard against her chest.

Her father had summoned her here. And she was wary of it.

She dropped onto the sofa across from him, her eyes fixed on her father. She felt like ten again, caught and waiting for his quiet wrath after some schoolyard slip.

He sat in his armchair, hands clamped on his knees as though he were holding something back. His face sported no discernible expression. No flicker of anger. No crease of sadness. His silence felt worse than any of his scoldings. It was a sign that she'd crossed a line he had not named.

"Kavya," he said at last, "we need to talk about this… situation."

Situation. That word landed like a stone in her heart, crushing her hope. Something cracked, something she could not mend. She held her tongue, knowing a fight wouldn't change his opinions. Not yet. Not when he'd already dug into Rudra.

"I've checked on this Rudra fellow," he went on. "What do you call him?"

Her stomach lurched. "Just Rudra, Baba," she forced her voice out.

He exhaled slowly, his stare pinning her down. "I don't like what I've found. Everything about him seems controversial. Some say he's mixed up in shady deals. Others say he's all power, no heart. Everyone warns he's trouble."

The room tilted around her as his words sank in. They sounded like a harsh final verdict that would brook no argument. She'd expected pushback, but not this. "What do you mean?" she croaked, voice trembling. "What'd they say?"

"He's unethical," he snapped. "Using politics for his own gain. Ambition over service. They've dealt with him, Kavya. Say he's a risk. Someone to steer clear of."

Her chest burned with a defiance she'd never thought she had in her. "That's not him, Baba," she shot back at her father. "He's kind… he's generous… he wants to lift people up. I know him."

"You're blind," he said. "Love's got you fooled. He's a politician. This means he'll bend anything to win. You're too soft to see it. And he'll break you."

She froze. His words felt like a blade twisted deep in her gut. Doubt crept in for a brief moment. She knew her father would have asked many people in the town. Could they all be wrong? If not, could she be wrong? However, she shook it off. "I don't know what to say," she murmured, "but I can't let him go. He's real to me."

Her father sighed. "I'm not happy, Kavya. He's not what I pictured for you. Not what I raised you for."

His disappointment hurt her. She started to grasp for a lifeline. "Mihir met him, Baba, and he liked him. He'll tell you. He's on my side."

His head shook. "I talked to Mihir. He's out. He won't back you. He sees it now."

Her knees buckled again. She felt as though the ground was about to give way below her. Mihir's defection hit her like a tight slap. Her brother. Her ally. Gone. Her father had sound arguments, and despite her love for Rudra, she felt powerless. She opened her mouth once but snapped it shut, looking out the window to watch the birds return to their nests.

Chapter 13

Tickets Confirmed

RUDRA sat on the couch as he listened to Kavya talking about what had transpired. Each word that came out of her mouth felt like a jagged shard that ripped through his heart. She recounted her father's inquiries about how he'd tracked down Rudra's Chachi through family connections. Her father had prodded and pried, digging into his life like a man unearthing an old tree's roots. The picture that had emerged came out warped. His chest tightened at listening to people badmouthing him. His knuckles whitened as he grasped his phone tightly.

"They don't know me," he thought. The realisation was as bitter as an unripe fruit. Like the rest of his family, his chachi did not really understand what he did. She couldn't grasp the nature of his job. And what she didn't understand, she denigrated.

Politics to people like her was a murky swamp. They distrusted it and viewed them as corrupt. They didn't know how intricately he danced between ideals and strategy. They didn't see the late nights he spent crafting narratives. They didn't see the victories he won through grit alone. They didn't notice the fire that drove him. Instead, they posted labels on him. Unstable, reckless, a man chasing ambition over duty. And they had handed this caricature to Kavya's father.

He felt a surge of frustration. He despised the game that society played. How they judged people's worth by wealth and titles! It didn't care for the unseen. His struggles, his vision, the way he'd carved his path—these things did not matter in their eyes. They always wanted proof. Something tangible to hold bright in the light.

It would not have mattered if their judgments had affected other aspects of his life, but their ignorant, petty opinions now seeped into his love for Kavya, poisoning what should have been pure.

The irony stung.

Rudra, the man everyone turned to for insights, the one who shaped stories and swayed minds, now had his life dissected by people who never bothered to look past the surface. He could almost hear the whispers, the sidelong jabs his chachi must have lobbed over a cup of chai. He's too ambitious, but there's no stability. What kind of husband would he be?

He refused to buckle. He had hoped he could still shift the tide. He trusted his strength, his determination, his clarity and purpose, and his faith in the love he bore for Kavya. He'd win them all over. Not with grand gestures, but with the truth of who he really was.

Picturing Kavya's father, he saw a man he respected despite the rift, sifting through rumours with a furrowed brow. He understood his instinct. The old man wasn't wrong to question. He just looked in the wrong places.

He felt a turmoil in her voice.

Mihir's backing out must have disheartened her, he told himself. Family could be a knotty thing.

That night, their call was brief. "We'll get through this," he murmured, more to himself than to her.

The next morning, they switched to video calls.

Kavya's face glowed on the screen, fatigue darkening the area around her eyes. Apparently, she'd spoken to her therapist, Indu, about the matter.

"What'd she say about me, bro?" he asked.

She smiled. "She said to keep things as they are. That we love each other, and that's what matters. She thinks you earn your way honestly. With talent. So nothing unethical about it."

He sighed with relief. Indu's words soothed his pride, confirming what he'd always known. Still, the word unethical troubled his mind.

Soon, they talked and laughed with each other. She told him she'd booked a ticket to Mumbai for the day after tomorrow. "Can you confirm them?" she asked.

He nodded and said he'd make it happen.

Politics had its perks, after all. A quick call resulted in a favour cashed in, and soon the tickets were secured.

She then launched into her plans. They included an exhibition next week with her designs on display.

"They're shipping out tomorrow morning," she said, her hands gesturing as if sketching the air. "It's going to be hectic."

They continued chatting throughout the day. Quick texts and a call before bed. "See you later, alligator," she teased.

"In a while, crocodile," he shot back playfully.

His heart ached with a love that transcended all barriers. They both knew the other person was feeling sad. But they chose to keep it aside and focus on the good things they had. They were so much stronger than this.

Kavya felt the familiar walls of her home closing in around her. She stood looking out the window, facing the sun in all its glory. Her heart felt cold despite the blistering heat. Thoughts of her father's odd questions about Rudra and their last call with each other churned in her mind. Her bones ached with weariness, and all she craved right now was quiet.

Fate seemed to have other plans, though. The doorbell rang shrilly, making her heart skip a beat. Opening the door, she found Sonakshi standing on the porchway. Dread claimed her chest just then. She had dodged this confrontation, but now her best friend stood on her doorstep. The confrontation was now inevitable. With a slow breath, she steeled herself and nodded at her friend.

Sonakshi's posture was still as a ruler, her silk blouse catching the light like liquid amber. Her keen and unyielding eyes locked onto Kavya's. A faint smirk played on her luscious lips.

Kavya understood its subtlety. It was triumph disguised as concern. Her stomach twisted just looking at her, but she didn't let her true feelings show.

"Sonakshi," she said, "what brings you here?"

Sonakshi breezed past her, heels clicking against the floor, her eyes roving about, trying to claim every inch of the space. "I came to check on you, Kavya," she replied. "Word got around of your father's little investigation. I just wanted to scc how you'rc holding up."

Kavya shut the door with a soft thud. She could smell the agenda in her best friend's mind. She had not just come here to check up on her. The timing of her arrival was no coincidence. She remembered that Rudra had taken her best friend out on a date once, and it had not gone well. Sonakshi was not one to let things go easily, especially if she felt slighted. "I'm fine," she said, folding her arms. "I just need some space right now."

Sonakshi slouched on the sofa, crossing her legs with the grace of a dancer. "I came all the way from Mumbai," she said, exasperated. "The least you can do is talk with me. Maybe over a cup of tea?"

Kavya bit back what she wanted to say. Irritation prickled under her skin. There was no escaping a conversation now. Sonakshi wouldn't just leave until she got what she wanted. She turned to the kitchen and started making the tea for both of them. When she returned, balancing two cups of tea, she handed one of them and sat on the sofa opposite her. Despite her behaviour, Sonakshi was still her friend. She had been with her through thick and thin. It was that which held her tongue.

"I'm still sorting through it all," she said. "So, what's this really about? Why are you here?"

Sonakshi sipped the tea, but her eyes never left Kavya. "I came to say I told you so," she said bluntly. "I saw this coming. Rudra's all ambition, power, and money. Your father's finally caught on and peeled back the mask. It's a good thing, Kavya. Time to let him go."

Heat flared in her chest. "I don't need a lecture," she snapped. "I know him… better than you ever will. You've always misjudged him. Always envied him. Just stay out of it."

Sonakshi laughed, her sound scraping Kavya's nerves raw. "Envious? I'm protecting you, Kavya. You deserve someone solid, someone who puts you first. Not a politician chasing his next win."

Kavya felt her eyes narrow. Her patience frayed like an old rope. "You don't know him," she retorted. "He's not this image you have built in your head. He's more than that."

"Oh, and you do?" Sonakshi countered. "You're drowning in a fantasy. Love's blinded you to the cracks, got you ignoring the truth. How will he hurt you? How he will always choose his career over you every freaking time!"

"You're wrong," Kavya said, her words hard like iron. "I see him… really see him. I love him, and he's mine. My choice, not yours."

"Fine," Sonakshi scoffed, standing abruptly, setting the teacup down. "Have it your way. But when he breaks you, when he proves me right, don't expect me to come pick up the pieces. I'm done trying."

She strode towards the door, leaving her tea half-finished.

Kavya stayed rooted to her spot, her best friend's words echoing in her ears, wishing she had at least one person in her corner.

Rudra heard his phone vibrate against the wooden table in front of him. He'd been waiting for Kavya's message and was glad to see her text flash on the screen.

KK: Boarded the train at 5:45. What time will you be free?

RR: Will be free by 8:30.

KK: Okay, I will be visiting Sonakshi first.

He felt his chest tighten.

Sonakshi. The name alone caused his heart to beat haphazardly. She was trouble, he had always known that. But he had to tolerate her. She was Kavya's best friend after all. Another message made his screen light up.

KK: Rudra, Dad texted Sonakshi.

Something cold crept up his spine, tightening the grip on his phone. What had her father said? What new thread unravelled here?

RR: Are you okay?

KK: I'll be fine in some time.

He could sense her sadness, making him want to shield her from everything that was going on. He longed for a day when they could be free of all this tension, when they would emerge whole together. He knew he had the strength in him, but was Kavya as strong? He hoped she didn't buckle under pressure.

RR: Bro, what's the plan? What time shall I see you?

KK: Rudra, can you pick me up from Sonakshi's at 9:15?

RR: Ok.

He'd be there. He'd reach early.

As promised to himself, he reached Sonakshi's five minutes early. Parking under a flickering streetlamp, he lit a cigarette, its embers glowing like a tiny defiant star. Smoke curled from the lit end, but the pastime did little to settle the jittery pulse in his veins as he watched for her. She appeared, striding towards him, suitcase and bag clutched tight. Rudra leaned out, taking her bag away from her and setting it on the back seat.

Kavya slid into the car, and he leaned over, pressing a lingering kiss on her cheek. He settled behind the wheel and pressed on the accelerator. The city blurred past, headlights cutting through the dark as they drove to his destination.

At their usual spot, they claimed a table and ordered some nachos. "Rudra, I felt suffocated at Sonakshi's," Kavya said. "I had gone there because Dad needed me to deliver something. And I went there despite things not being good between me and me. She had friends over. She was having a house party. I couldn't do it." She clasped his hands. "This… you… are what I needed."

He smiled and brushed a kiss across her nose. "You've got this pull, Kavya," he murmured. "You always steal every ounce of me."

Their lips puckered in a playful dance and then parted as the nachos arrived. Halfway through, they ordered drinks and a pizza. Her insistence on having pineapple on it made him look at her askance. It was a quirk he didn't understand but adored.

They devoured the pizza, though he let Kavya have the pineapple slices. He queued up their songs, 'Words' and 'You Say It Best When You Say Nothing At All' from Notting Hill. The melodies comforted them. As they ate and sipped, his gaze drifted to a woman at the front table, her laugh catching his ear. Kavya nudged him gently, pulling him back. Her eyes looked at him with mock reproach. "Eyes on me, bro," she teased, though her tone carried an edge.

Heat crept up his neck, making him fumble, reaching for her hand. "I wasn't really looking," he said, defending himself.

She smiled.

He vowed to tame his wandering gaze.

Before leaving, they ordered pasta, which was her favourite, and then he steered the conversation to safer ground. "So, what did Sonakshi say?" he asked.

"I'll tell you tomorrow," she replied, her tone a plea to let the matter rest.

"Are you worried?" he pressed.

"No, Rudra, I'm good now. I just missed you."

"I love you," he said, tender and sure.

"I love you too," she echoed.

They left the restaurant hand in hand. "Isharon Isharon main" split from the speakers as they drove home. Once inside, he wrapped her in a tight embrace. He plucked the stick from her bun and placed it on the table. He kissed her again, lips hungry and seeking. Their passion flared. A wildfire consumed his body as he led her to the bed and shed his clothes while watching her do the same. They both changed into comfortable nightwear.

They tumbled into the bed with her head nestling on his arm. They kept staring at each other until sleep finally claimed them.

The next morning, Rudra woke first and looked at her first thing. Her beauty stole his breath away. He pulled her close, his lips grazing her soft skin, and their bodies entwined now in a rhythm that matched their heartbeats.

Sunday unfolded slowly and sweetly. They ordered breakfast after a playful debate. His love for hearty plates clashed with her lighter tastes. "Life's a Sunday morning," her bio read.

He let her choose.

She shook her head. "Get all the junk you want," she said, mischief glinting in her eyes.

He placed a bountiful order. Pav bhaji, matar kulcha, bhel puri, dabelis, and a fiery dosa. The food tasted mediocre, but they ate with laughter and love, so they forgot the taste.

"Rudra, you're banned from ordering," she quipped. "You never finish anything."

He chuckled, happy to hand her the reins. He'd always hated the chore, anyway.

"I think he'll come around," she said, hope tinged in her voice. And then abruptly, she demanded, "Rudra, I want chocolates and a Biscoff biscuit."

It was a distraction, he knew, but he ordered them anyway. His heart twisted as she devoured two packs of Nutties. She didn't offer him even one, although she did share the biscuit with him.

As she munched, she spun a tale of Dadi's wisdom and respect.

"Maybe talk to her if your dad continues to hold out," he suggested. "Maybe she could sway him."

Kavya fell silent.

He let it drop, curling around her instead. His fingers teased her hair and then her spectacles and then her bun. And then he remembered. He went to the dressing table and removed from the drawers a gift wrapped in red. She tore the wrapper open with glee and found a golden bun stick inside. "This is so beautiful," she muttered, her face lit up. "I'll wear it."

Rudra saw her tighten her bun and place the golden bun stick. It looked beautiful on her.

"I told you in the beginning I'd gift you this. It really looks beautiful."

He had placed an order for two bun sticks, both from different companies. The one he had really loved had not been delivered, and he was on the warpath with the company. The company's customer care had assured him swift delivery soon, but he didn't want to wait for it to come. So, he had wrapped the one he had received and gifted it to her. Looking at her glowing face made him happy. She would be happier when she got the other bun stick.

"You know what," he recklessly blurted out, "I made out with your juniors in school thirteen years back."

He'd meant it as a joke, but it looked like she was hurt.

"You can't just say this," she whispered, tapping his arm.

Guilt flooded him. "Sorry, bro, I was trying to lighten the mood. 'It was nothing, just kid stuff… Don't cry, please."

Her smile returned. It was faint, but real.

He kissed her again, on the cheek at first and then on the mole on her nose next, promising never to hurt her again.

She shifted her trip to Nashik to Tuesday morning, lying to her father that she had some work at the studio, and they savoured the extra night they got to spend with each other. At 5:30, hunger struck, and she ordered biscuit paratha and chole. The food was decent, but not so remarkable. They ate, talked, and napped all day. And then she had a sudden urge to cut his hair.

Dressed in a maroon shirt and baggy pyjamas, she led him to a popular salon franchise. He sat as the barber worked while she tasked the latter with her instructions. When it was done, she beamed. "Perfect," she said.

As they walked to have their food, Sonakshi's text interrupted her. Her father wanted a word.

Kavya's call was brief, and they turned towards another restaurant, where they could have some healthy food options. They ordered ragi golgappas, millet soup, and jackfruit salad. It was healthy and bland.

Another call pulled her outside, and when she returned, she was quieter and more distant. They ate, paid, and then he drove her away, with her sleeping through the ride. At home, he kissed her awake. "Baby, we're here."

They collapsed onto the bed and slept through the rest of the night.

At 5:15 A.M., he woke up and kissed her forehead. "I love you," she whispered.

"Love you more, bro," he replied.

He drove her to the station and watched her disappear through the gate. His heart ached for her, but he promised himself he'd see her soon.

Chapter 14

Turbulence 2.0

KAVYA searched for a way to change her father's mind, finding ways to plead her case. But even her heartfelt words proved inadequate for her father to be less stubborn about his decision. He didn't even reply to her. The man who'd once hoisted her on his shoulders appeared distant and tense, making plain his suspicion about the two nights she had spent with Rudra.

Her phone buzzed that instant. Her pulse quickened, thinking it was Rudra, but the screen unfortunately flashed Sonakshi's name. She hadn't spoken to Sonakshi for days and had no appetite for her meddling. That woman had a knack for slithering into her life uninvited. Especially now because of the spite she harboured for Rudra. Spite for him rejecting her and preferring Kavya. She, however, decided to face the storm rather than ignore it.

"Sonakshi, what do you want?" she asked, irritated. "I'm not in the mood for more trouble."

"Well, I came to see your father today, actually," she answered. "So maybe we can talk in person, no?"

Her heart beat faster as she heard those words. Why did Sonakshi want to meet her father? Was it about Rudra?

Her friend thrived on stirring the pot when she felt like it, and now she'd brought her chaos right on her doorstep. She crossed over to the front door, having noticed Sonakshi's car pull up the driveway, and swung it open. Sonakshi stood there, framed by the porchlight's halo, her silk blouse shimmering like a predator's scales.

Kavya felt her stomach lurch.

"Sonakshi, what do you want?" she repeated.

Sonakshi breezed past her. "Told you… I came to meet your father, Kavya, to discuss Rudra," she said. "He'll need more information, you know. I'm just helping out."

A frown encroached on her forehead. Why was she so interested in destroying her love life?

Footsteps thudded from the hall, and her father emerged from his study, his face like a quietened storm. His eyes flicked to Sonakshi.

Kavya breathed deep, knowing full well that he prized Sonakshi's word and trusted her like he would a second daughter. It was a bond that Kavya now cursed silently.

"Hello, Uncle," Sonakshi greeted him with aplomb.

"Hello, beta," her father replied. "So, what did you want to discuss?"

Kavya felt her breath hitch. Her father had gotten right to the point.

Sonakshi pivoted to her father, her smile turning predatory. "Well, Uncle, as I mentioned over the phone, I wanted to share some information about Rudra," she said. "I've heard some concerning things."

Her heart plummeted, her hands clenching into fists. Why was this Sonakshi so interfering?

Sonakshi fished her phone from her bag and swiped the phone, opening a few photos with a flourish. Images of Rudra flickered into view, laughing with two people who looked more like thugs. The photo angles twisted them into something sinister. The shadows in the dark alley sharpened their features, cigarettes glowed like warning flares, and their casual grins morphed into something menacing.

"These are Rudra meeting... some of his... ahem.... associates," Sonakshi said, stuttering. "I've heard these two are violent, with ties to the underworld. You should know the company he keeps."

Kavya felt the room spinning under her feet. Shock and fury crashed over her in that instant. She had always known Rudra's world was full of grit. These photos were definitely manipulated using Photoshop. A lie spun from truth.

Her father, though, could not tell an original photo from its digital distortion. His face hardened, eyes full of rage. "What's this, Kavya?" he demanded in an icy tone. "Who are these people? You swore he was ethical."

There was an accusing stare in his eyes that made her back away a little. It was as if she'd woven a web of deceit to snare his trust. Her knees trembled, but she held her ground. Sonakshi's words had sunk their claws into her father's worst fears. She scrambled for a defence, but she really did not have any answers.

Sonakshi turned to her, like a victor savouring the spoils. "You should've listened, Kavya. I told you he wasn't right for you. Now I've proven it. For your sake. I couldn't let you get hurt by a man like that."

She knew what she was telling was all fake, but she had no words to say to her.

Sonakshi turned to her father again. "I know you want what's best for Kavya, Uncle. I had to show you his true colours since she wouldn't hear me out. I did this to save her from making a mistake."

Her father swung to her, disappointed.

Kavya wanted to fight back, but her tongue lay cold. For now, they had the upper hand. She had no answers to their questions. What this all meant for her relationship with Rudra, she could not say. But this was sure. Sonakshi had crushed her hope tonight.

At any other time, Rudra would have called the campaign a hive of activity. Today, though, it felt flat. Campaign posters in their faded form felt stuck to the walls, letters lay haphazardly on the tables, ink bleeding into coffee stains. He waded through the mess, phone pressed to his ears, finding it challenging to hear the tiny voice on the other end of the line because of the chatter of the aides and the clatter of keyboards. His mind churned through many topics. There were a lot of tasks that demanded his attention now that the elections neared.

He had been working tirelessly, organising community meetings with the leaders of the artisans, listening to their grievances, their concerns, their fears, trying to find a solution to the problem that was affecting their livelihoods. He had felt their frustration, their helplessness, their sense of being forgotten, a mirror to his own emotions, a reminder of the need to make change, to fight for the rights of the marginalised. He knew that these protests were not just about economic grievances; they were a reflection of a deeper systemic failure, of the long and painful battles that the small-scale business owners were forced to endure. And he wanted to help them. For days now, he'd thrown himself into the fray. He'd sat on threadbare rugs with the artisan leaders who had a lot to say about the truck protests hampering their businesses. He'd sat through nasty smells of sweat and damp earth, listening to their woes. Their orders were drying up, the prices were plummeting, and their families teetered on the edge of poverty. He could feel their helplessness, just as he was helpless where Kavya was concerned.

Their cries weren't just monetary woes. They were battle cries against a system that had turned its back on the small-scale industries. He wondered what had happened for the party to ignore these people. After all, they were a potential vote bank. But a lot of their problems would be solved if the transport protests came to an end. While some transport had resumed, not everything was. The state was in a tense situation, and the media circled them like vultures.

He'd burned the midnight oil over many reports, each statistic a plea he couldn't ignore. Today, though, a new shadow loomed. Harish had called him and told him he wished to meet.

The door banged open, and Harish stormed in, his shirt rumpled, eyes wild with the glint of a man who'd unearthed something big.

Rudra dropped the phone mid-sentence and straightened. He knew Harishbhai didn't waste time with pleasantries.

"Boss, you're not going to believe this," Harish said. "Those union leaders? The ones stirring up the protests out by the depots? They're not just pissed-off haulers."

His brows furrowed. He had suspected this, but he wanted confirmation. "Spit it out, Harish. What'd you dig up?"

"I got a tip from a guy who knows a guy. Deep in the weeds, right? These bastards are on someone's payroll. Someone with deep pockets is playing them. And there's a Naxalite connection to this. Straight out of East Maharashtra. They aren't just blocking roads for better rates. They're trying to choke the state. Bring the whole damn economy to its knees so the opposition can use it for the elections."

The words hit Rudra like a fist straight to his sternum. The protest leaders were pawns in a political game. "Naxalites?" he echoed. "Are you sure?"

"Dead sure!" Harish asserted. "Got names, dates... My guys even traced a couple of their runners back to Gadchiroli.

They aren't hauling goods. They're creating chaos. Violence is their ticket, boss. They want control, and they're using these poor sods to light the fuse."

His jaw clenched.

The state was now a tinderbox. This was no random spark.

He saw the bigger picture now. Shadowy figures pulling strings, sowing discord to reap power, their hands stained with more than just dirt.

"Get me everything," he said. "Every scrap you got. Photos, contacts, whatever the tipster coughed up. We're taking this to the party office tonight."

Harish grinned, flashing his feral teeth. "Already on it. I'll have a dossier by sundown. Thick enough to choke 'em with. You gonna roast the bastards or what?"

Rudra's lips twitched. "I'll do more than just roast them. I'll rip their whole damn plan apart. Show the state who's really bleeding for it." He turned and put on his jacket. "And, Harishbhai, keep your ear to the ground. They'll move fast once they smell us coming."

Harish nodded, already halfway out the door.

Rudra stood alone for a moment, the din in the office fading to the background. Kavya's face flashed before him, and he remembered that his purpose was to do better by the community. He grabbed his keys and walked out into the early evening with nothing to say to the other volunteers.

Chapter 15

Maybe It's an End

HARISH flipped the cover open, his thick fingers jabbing at the photo on the top. It was that of a wiry man with a scar snaking down his cheek, caught mid-handshake with another figure covered in shadow. Rudra's pulse throbbed in his ears like a steady war drum as he locked eyes with the campaign manager.

"Sir, we've got something," Rudra said, his voice louder than the rickety noise of the fan overhead. He jerked his chin at Harish, who stepped forward and slammed the dossier onto the manager's desk. The force sent a pen skittering to the ground. He could hear Harish apologising profusely. But it was not just the pen that dropped down. Papers fanned out too. Photos containing dark secrets. Grainy stills of the transport leaders hunched over tables, cigarette smoke curling around their heads.

"This is Prakash," Harish growled. "Leads the protests out east. He's a front tied to the Naxalites out of Gadchiroli." The manager leaned forward. "Naxalites?" he rumbled. "This better be more than a hunch, Harish."

"Oh, I've got more," Harish said as he dug deeper into the file. He yanked out a thumb drive and tossed it onto the desk. "That's two hours of video there. I'll summarise. Prakash and his crew are meeting runners in some hinterland dhaba, passing envelopes, plotting roadblocks. Voices are muffled, but you can hear 'disrupt' and 'control' clear as day." He tapped a stack of bank statements next, their yellowed edges curling. "Then there's this… these are the financials. Shell companies, three layers deep, funnelling cash to Prakash and his lieutenants. My guys traced a chunk back to an outfit in East Maharashtra. Not airtight yet, but it stinks of Naxal money."

Rudra breathed deep as the manager sifted through the dossier, his hands flipping through the photos. A truck convoy stalled on a dusty highway. Men in faded kurtas shouting with fists raised. A blurry shot of a ledger with numbers written in red ink. He stepped closer. "It's not complete, Sir," he said, "but it's enough. They're not just mad about the diesel prices. They're choking the state. Sabotage dressed up as protests. The government can move on this. Raids, arrests, whatever it takes."

The manager grunted and rubbed his jaw. "Messy," he muttered, "but a start nonetheless. Enough to rattle a few cages. But you sure of this, kid? Stirring this pot means blowback… of the ugly kind."

Rudra met his gaze and did not flinch. "I'm sure. The people… they're bleeding out there. We let this fester, and it's not just the economy that collapses. It'll be them."

The manager nodded. "Alright. I'll take this upstairs and get the wheels turning. But you two keep digging. I want every loose end tied before the shit hits the fan." He scooped up the dossier and waved them out.

Rudra stepped into the hall, Harish at his flank. "You'd better be careful," he warned.

Harish nodded. "You too, Rudrabhai."

Rudra stumbled into his apartment, his legs itching for release. So, he laced up his sneakers and ran into the night. Pavement blurred under his feet as he pushed hard. He tore through a 5K in twenty-eight minutes. Sweat stung his eyes. His lungs scorched as if he could outrun the storm brewing inside him. The city's humidity clung to his skin, but the chaotic voices in his head refused to quieten down.

Back home, chest heaving, he collapsed onto the floor, legs splayed on the cool tiles. His body screamed for rest, but his mind busied itself with many thoughts. He dragged himself into a cross-legged slump and slowed down his breathing. Forty minutes of pranayama slipped by, air hissing through his nose. The clock's hands crept past ten when he finished.

A hollow ache started to pain him from the inside. He needed to hear her voice. He needed to know she was still his.

He dialled Kavya's number.

She picked up his call pretty quickly.

"Are you home yet?" he asked.

"Rudra, on my way home," she replied.

Worry coiled in his gut. He wanted to ask the questions he wanted. Was she okay? Was she still with him? He bit them back, though. "Did you speak with Sonakshi?" he questioned instead.

"Yes," she said, clipped and hurt.

"So, what'd she say?"

"Rudra, I'll reach home and call you," she answered.

"Okay," he murmured.

The line went dead.

He hauled himself up and showered in a rush. Hot water took away the sweat as it drained into the sink, but the unease lingered. He ate some toast and drank some chai. And then he waited until the morning. But the call did not come.

When the morning came, he had a heavy breakfast and drove towards his office. The drive turned out to be long as the roads showed heavy traffic. Halfway to the office, he called her again.

She picked up his call, and when she spoke, her voice sounded brittle and stressed. "Rudra, Dad's not cool about us being together," she said. "He hasn't slept well since I told him about you." She was pained; that much was evident.

He sucked in a breath. "I know, Kavya, we said we'd give him time before bringing it up again," he said, still hopeful. "We'll figure it out together."

"Rudra, we'll talk about this tonight," she cut in, sounding resigned.

"Okay," he said.

The call ended.

His hands clutched the wheel tightly.

Kavya's loyalty to her family was a strong thread he'd admired. Now the same thread threatened to sever them. He couldn't begrudge her, but the thought of losing her made him anxious.

When he came to the office, it swallowed him in a slate of meetings and handshakes. But he did not forget her or to text her.

RR: Don't worry. Everything will be fine. Things will fall into place.

KK: Rudra, I don't think it will.

He frowned. What had happened for Kavya to lose out on hope? Had Sonakshi said something? He didn't respond. He decided to give her some space. But he wouldn't let her go without a stand. They'd planned to talk that evening, so he waited.

The day unravelled. A meeting stretched two hours past its limit, last-minute crises piling up like a storm. He fired off an apology text.

RR: Running late, sorry.

He then drove towards Nashik, having promised his mother that he'd visit.

When he called her again that night, her voice sounded like a ghost. Faint and worn, evidence of tears she'd already shed.

"Kavya, we'll sort this out, don't worry… I love you," he urged, wanting to pull her back from the brink.

"No, Rudra, I think we should call this off," she whispered. Each word in that sentence fell like a blow to his heart. "I can't take it. I can't watch Dad unravel like this. Without his blessing, I won't go further."

"Kavya, don't lose hope," he reasoned. "Give it a month or two. We'll try again. We'll fix this." He said that in a pleading tone, recounting their late-night talks, the way their hands fit in each other's. But she seemed firm and resolute in her decision on the other end. Like a wall he couldn't break. The Kavya who took a stand and fought was not there anymore. He wouldn't beg or grovel. "It's okay if you want to end things," he snapped finally. He regretted the tone instantly. But the hurt in his heart roared louder.

"Rudra, we can stay as friends," she offered.

"No… I can't," he rasped. "I can't just be your friend, Kavya. I don't know how to unlove you."

The idea scorched him. He'd rather burn than fade into that half-light. How had all of this unravelled so fast? Hours ago, they were planning their future. Now, it lay in ashes.

"Take care, Kavya," he murmured, barely holding it together. "I'll try not to call."

Her cries followed him as he disconnected.

The drive blurred past, his mind full of questions that had no answers. Had her father turned her? Had

Sonakshi struck the killing blow? Was their love too fragile? Or was he?

He pulled into the driveway. His mother welcomed him into the house, but she sensed his worry.

"What happened, beta?" she asked, her hand brushing his cheek.

"For the first time. Ma, I know what real sadness feels like," he whispered.

She drew him close without asking him another question. "Don't worry… we're here," she said. "God bless you."

When the dawn arrived the next day, he woke up with a chest feeling like a stone weight. Habit urged him to use his phone to call her, but he fought it. Rolling out of bed, he laced up the sneakers again and ran eleven kilometres with his legs pumping like pistons. But no matter how much he ran, he couldn't outrun his grief. His breath tore free in ragged gasps by the time he reached home. And, after, he spent the rest of the day eating, sleeping, and moving through the daily motions. Night fell early that day, and with a single tear racing down his cheek, he sank into his bed with a bruised heart.

He woke up at dawn again, and as usual, his habit once again suggested he call her. But he was stuck in a sea of contradictions; he didn't know how to get out of it.

Headlights made his skull pulse as Rudra drove through the grey haze of Mumbai's traffic-laden streets. He gripped the wheel tightly and dialled Kavya's number. His fingers shook as he waited for her to pick up his call. She answered, her voice strained, as though she had been waiting for the call. It felt for a while that they had returned to their old habits, but their efforts were failing miserably. They talked for twenty whole minutes. Their conversation used to be lively once upon a time, but now the energy had been replaced by pain. There was a wide chasm between them now, a gaping hole they could not fill.

He staggered into his apartment and went to bed early. Sleep was his only refuge, hoping to escape the pain that had become a constant companion. His parents offered him sympathy, but he didn't want to face their pity. He began to crave the dark and the solitude that came with it.

At half past three in the morning, he awoke with a gasp, his eyes noticing the faint red glow of the digital clock hung upon the wall. Panic clawed up his throat as he thought more and more about Kavya. He fumbled for a glass and then gulped water down his throat as though there was a raging fire in his gut. He tried to meditate after. It had worked to calm him down before, but now his mind spun wild. What if she'd gone for good? What if he had pushed too hard? He kept chanting under his breath, but the storm inside him wouldn't relent. Defeated, he slumped against the wall, eyes shut, tears breaking free. His armour had finally cracked.

He stayed like that until dawn crept in, painting the room in thin golden slivers. He rose, his heart heavy from all the rancid thoughts. He dialled her number again, hands shivering, but she didn't answer. One time. Two times. Three times. No answer.

RR: Kavya, call me.

His eyes looked at his own text. It was the first time, perhaps, that he had ditched her nickname.

Sleep dodged him, and he waited until the clock rang seven. Impatience won again.

He dialled her number. This time, she answered. "Rudra, I just woke up," she said, her voice as distant as a stranger's echo.

"You back to putting your phone on DND?" he asked.

"Yes," she replied, confirming the wall she had put up between him and her.

He was sure something had happened. Perhaps Sonakshi had twisted her against me. Maybe someone had whispered lies into her ears. Or was there another guy?

"Kavya, you said once that I made you feel special," he pressed. "Every moment we had, you felt it. So, why are we doing this? Why end something this good?"

"I can't go against Dad," she answered in a resigned voice. "He will not budge. I know him."

"We'll talk to him again," Rudra insisted, still clinging to hope. "We can—"

"No point," she interrupted. "He won't agree." A beat of silence followed. "Rudra, let's not talk about this."

The call fizzled out, and he sat on the bed, the line dead in his hand. A few days passed like that. They resisted calling each other. She, most of all. And then, all of a sudden, a text from her made his phone buzz.

KK: Dad's BP went high today. He won't let this happen. I won't be able to speak with you regularly from now on. I've had the best time with you, and I wish you all the best.

There was a finality to those words he could not shake so easily. It was like a door slamming shut.

RR: It's okay, Kavya. Take care of your dad and let me know if you need any help. I'm just a call away.

For three days, he resisted calling her. He dragged himself through work and family dinners. Yet, she never vanished from his mind. On the fourth day, he caved in and called her again.

"How's your dad?" he asked.

"He's fine, Rudra," she replied. She fell silent for a brief moment before she said, "We've got to stop. Or it'll be harder for us both."

"I can't bury how I feel," he said, showing his vulnerability. "And you shouldn't either."

"I can't keep doing this," she murmured, a plea wrapped in goodbye.

"Okay, Kavya," he said, defeated. "I won't call again."

Once the call ended, sleep came fitfully with her face haunting his dreams.

He woke at midnight with tears streaming down his cheek. He prayed into the dark, begging for a sign. He wanted a miracle to happen just then. He wished for fate to stitch them together. Dawn brought no answers. Just a restless urge. He scrolled through Instagram. Her story had details of an exhibition in Rajkot. His pulse surged. He had to see her.

Before deciding, he thought he should get his sister's point of view. He drove to his sister's house, and as expected, she lay calm on the living room couch with a book. Her sharp eyes met his as soon as he entered through the open door. "Rashmi," he started, "Kavya's slipping away. Her dad's against us. And she's letting go. I don't know what to do."

She set her book down and stood up to face him. "Rudra, you're a mess, but you're not blind. You love her. You really do. That's rare." She tapped his chest. "Follow your heart, bhai. Don't let her father's shadow snuff it out. Persevere. Show up for her, even if she pushes back. You've always fought for what matters. Don't stop now."

He nodded. Her words had ignited a spark in him again. "She'll be in Rajkot soon. I could go there."

"Then go," Rashmi urged. "Be there. Let her see you're not giving up. You'll regret it if you don't."

Those words sealed it.

Rajkot called out to him. He would go there. Not to beg, but to be in her orbit. To prove their story wasn't finished as she thought. He hauled himself up and planned his tickets. He'd fight for her. He'd not let their love end in silence and surrender. Losing her was not an option he could live with.

Chapter 16

Vriksha Art Gallery

RUDRA slouched in the worn armchair in Dr Harsha's office, the faint hum of traffic on the streets annoying him. Back in 2022, when he'd walked in here last, it was on a whim. He had a rare self-realisation that had prodded him into speaking with a counsellor to address some unresolved issues. The session hadn't panned out the way he had expected; its lessons were buried in the grind of work. Now, two years later, he sat here again to talk about his issues with Kavya.

Dr Harsha sat across from him, her ageing silver hair tied behind in a braid, her eyes a patient cesspool of wisdom. Sitting there, Rudra started to spill his entire story, starting with the early days of his relationship with Kavya, their first meeting where he was late, and how he had gone on multiple dates after. He then shared their common traits and different habits, how their romance progressed, and then how the fracture happened. He explained to her about her father's disapproval and his struggle with her absence. Dr Harsha, on the other hand, listened to him with rapt attention.

When he mentioned Rajkot and his plan to crash her exhibition, her lips quirked. "You should go, Rudra," she advised. "Follow that pull. See where you both stand." Her words now stoked the fire in his heart. His sister had told him the same thing. Both of them got it. His longing for her. His need to fight for what he'd lost.

"I'll book the tickets tomorrow," he said, resolute. "Thanks, Dr Harsha."

The session ended with him stepping out into the humid night. A strange kind of calm seeped into him. His anxiety had lessened by half. Maybe more than half. The counsellor hadn't waved a magic wand or something. Just narrating his story to her made him realise he was on the right side of things. Going home, he drifted into sleep where he dreamed of her as he always did.

When morning broke, he lunged for his phone to book his flight tickets to Ahmedabad. It was Rajkot's closest hub, three hours by road. Friends had pushed for a direct train, but he wanted speed. Direct flights to Rajkot had been booked solid, so Ahmedabad was his only shot.

Would she really be there? Would she turn him away? What if her father were with her? Each question felt like a thorn in his side. He swatted the questions aside in his mind, focusing on the positives.

He had to see her. He had to know.

He spent the rest of the day resting, and when night came, he slept as early as he possibly could. When dawn came, he hit the gym, muscles straining against iron, sweat beading on his brow. Breakfast followed soon after the gym session, consisting of parathas heavy with homemade ghee. He mapped his moves, shoving his emotions to the side. He first dialled Gaurav, his rock of a friend, and laid it out to him. "She's at an exhibition in Rajkot, September 10th. Can you confirm she'll be there? Timings? Everything?"

"On it, bro," Gaurav said, without hesitating. "Tulika will handle it. My dear wife speaks awesome Gujarati and knows how to dig."

As Gaurav had said, his wife was a force. Her call to the gallery had been swift. She rang back minutes later. "Kavya's there both days. 11 A.M. to 7 P.M. You're good."

He sighed, relieved.

His plan snapped into focus in his mind. He'd show her his fight, his love, his all.

His flight was set for 8:55 A.M. in the morning. Ahmedabad to Rajkot is a tight sprint after. He spent the rest of the day ticking boxes. Car rental, hotel reservations, and a mental recreation of her face when she'd see him. That night, he met a buddy, shared a cigarette under a streetlamp, and then crashed home again. He jolted awake at 2 A.M., restless. Meditation flopped a second time, much to his surprise. He kept pacing across the room, the floorboards creaking as he did. Sleep kept a distance away, so he lay staring at the ceiling's cracked veins, picturing everything about her.

At half past two, he gave up and called his driver. "Be here by 4:15," he barked. He then soaked himself in a long bath, steam fogging the bathroom mirror. Pulling on a crisp shirt, he nudged Beena Didi awake. "Aloo parathas for me. Two for me. Two for my driver. Quick."

She grumbled but complied. He started to stuff clothes, a toothbrush, moisturising cream, shampoo, and other essentials into a black bag.

Soon, Beena Didi announced that the parathas were ready. Breakfast went down fast. And when the driver came, he handed over a couple of parathas to him and said, "Eat up!"

After the driver had wolfed his share, they rolled out at ten past five. Even though the city was still half-asleep, Rudra felt excited like a live wire. They reached the airport an hour later.

He walked through the morning airport crowd and checked in. Seeing a shop, a whim struck him. He ducked into the shop, where he grabbed chocolates, gum, and a sharp deodorant.

A small announcement made his ear prickle. The flight had been delayed by half an hour.

He swore under his breath and sank into a plastic chair.

Dr Harsha's number flared up on his phone as he scrolled through his contact list. He dialled the number, craving her steadying hand. "I'm going," he said, his voice tight. "But what if it's too much?"

"Don't push her," she said. "Just be there. Share the air. Feel it out. No pressure."

After her call, he arranged a bouquet of white lilies, phoning a vendor to hit the gallery by half past two. Boarding came at 9:25. He settled into his seat, eager to see her. Seventy minutes stretched ahead. He pulled out his phone and spilt his soul into the notes. Kavya filled every line of it. Every beat. He flew towards her, certain he'd fight for her till the end.

The plane touched down at 10:35 A.M. in Ahmedabad. The plane's wheels screeched against the tarmac, jarring his bones. His heart pounded against his chest. With just a small bag slung over his shoulder, he breezed through the terminal, shoving past bleary-eyed travellers to the exit. Gaurav had arranged a cab for him. It idled there, a battered white sedan glinting under the Gujarat sun. Rudra climbed into it at 11 sharp.

"How long to Rajkot?" he asked.

"Three and a half hours, maybe? Four also?" The driver replied, eyes flicking to the rearview.

He groaned. He wondered if he could wait that long. Google Maps blinked an ETA of three hours and fifteen minutes. It was a sliver of hope, but still too damn far.

"Make it quick," he urged.

The cab lurched onto the highway. His mind raced ahead, painting her in his arms. It was a reunion he ached for since she'd slipped away.

Thirty minutes in, his stomach growled. Hungry, he tapped the driver on his shoulder. "Pull over somewhere to eat."

They veered towards a roadside dhaba, its tin roof glinting like a bright beacon. He ordered a plate of sabzi and roti. Though it was a light, quick, and steadying bite, he wolfed it down, the flavours melting on his tongue. By half past twelve in the afternoon, he stood outside, smoking a cigarette. Five minutes later, they roared back onto the road.

The expressway unfurled half an hour later. The ETA now ticked down to two hours and forty. "Drive fast, bhaiyya," he pressed, sounding desperate.

"This is a taxi, sahib," the driver shot back, a wry twist in his voice. "Speed's capped—can't push past it."

Rudra huffed, frustration bubbling up, hot and sour. "Try anyway," he muttered, eyes tracing the horizon, willing the miles to shrink. Then he sank back, lids dropping, surrendering to a nap.

He jolted awake at 1:10, forty minutes gone. The ETA glared: one hour forty-five. "Go faster, bhaiyya," he growled, needing to claw at him.

The driver's same dry excuse came. "Speed's fixed, sahib."

Annoyed, he yanked out his phone and dialled Gaurav. "Talk to this guy. Get him to speed up," he said.

Gaurav's calm voice worked its magic. The driver grumbled but floored it, the engine's whine rising like a battle cry.

Rudra shut his eyes again, gathering strength, and woke up at half past two as Rajkot's dusty, sun-bleached welcome sign loomed. The gallery lay thirty-four kilometres away, fifty minutes still. He felt her near.

He rang the flower vendor. "Bouquet, forty-five minutes sharp."

At 3:15, they rolled past Vishwanath Temple, its spires piercing the sky. His stomach fluttered, butterflies rioting. Five hundred meters from her, his heartbeat thundered. He leapt out, darting inside the temple. Kneeling before the deity, he clasped his hands and prayed.

Back in the cab, he dialled the vendor again. "Five minutes? Good."

At half past three, the bouquet landed in his hands.

"Call her," he told the driver in a hushed voice, dictating her number. "Say a parcel's coming in ten. See how she reacts." He scribbled a note. Good luck, bro. In a while, crocodile. His signature sign-off.

The driver trotted off.

He stepped out and smoked a cigarette as he watched the gallery's glass doors. He saw her come out and take the bouquet, though she didn't check his note. Patience thinned inside him, but he'd wait. She'd test him, but he'd endure.

Just as he finished his cigarette, she emerged from the gallery and noticed him standing. "Rudra!" she called out, surprise lifting her voice.

He strode towards her with sure steps, eyes locked on hers. "Bro!" he shouted with joy.

Her smile widened, tears glinting like stars. "Come upstairs," she said, waving to him.

The lift hummed. With every floor it climbed, he remembered the time he spent with her. It flashed before his eyes until the doors parted.

She stood there outside, radiant, smiling like she'd waited for him all along, stealing his breath. "Rudra, why are you here?" she asked, voice trembling with disbelief, eyes brimming. "I can't believe this…"

He closed the gap, arms wrapping her tight. His chin rested on her head. "I love you, Kavya. I feel you right here." They clasped hands, gazes tangled, lost in a bubble of their own.

She tugged him into the gallery, eager to unveil her work. Bangles, necklaces, and designs of her own making. "Three hours left," she said, nudging him toward a corner chair. "Sit there."

He slumped into it, tension melting. She handed him water, fingers brushing his, eyes lingering. "Is this real?" she whispered, half-laughing.

"It's real," he said, conviction steady as stone. "With me, it always will be."

Pride swelled inside him as he saw her deal with potential customers, turning them into buyers. He met Anuradha, the gallery owner, whose warm words appreciating Kavya's talent, then settled back, gaze fixed on her. Distance hadn't dulled their fire—it blazed brighter.

"One last task," she said, turning to him, "then coffee. After, I'll tweak the cost sheet, and we'll grab dinner."

They left the gallery together at 7:00 and entered a nearby coffee shop. She flipped open her laptop, fingers flying over keys, multitasking with a grace he'd always envied. He sipped his drink, watching her. The ache of weeks spent apart faded, replaced by a certainty that this, her, was home.

"Rudra," Kavya called, her eyes pinning him from across the table. "Why'd you come here when you know it's over? Don't you think that's wrong?"

He met her stare, a slow smile tugging his lips, defiance flickering beneath his calm. "I wanted to," he said, voice steady, belying the storm churning inside. "I couldn't fight it. And for the next two days, let's skip the 'whys.' I just want this—us, right now."

Her lips curved into a faint smile.

She leaned across, pressing a kiss to his cheek, and returned to whatever she was doing.

Once her tasks were completed, they wandered out into Rajkot's dusk. Rudra clutched her bag, its worn strap rough against his palm. At a Gujarati restaurant's threshold, their eyes locked. There was doubt in her eyes. Regardless, they stepped inside, a strong smell of turmeric wafting in his nose. They ordered thalis, silver trays gleaming under dim lights, but the comfort Rudra usually found in the spiced dal and warm rotis eluded him tonight.

"Rudra, we shouldn't do this," Kavya said, voice trembling. "It'll hurt us both."

His chest ached at her distress. He wanted to shield her from everything. "Kavya, I don't want to hash it out now," he replied, firm but gentle. "This moment—it's enough. Let me stay with you tonight." Her nearness was all he craved.

"No, Rudra, it's not right," she countered, her tone caught between longing and duty, a tug-of-war he felt in his bones.

"I've got a lot to say," he said, voice resolute, "but not yet."

"Okay," she murmured.

Silence draped over their meal, heavy and unspoken, though Rudra clung to a stubborn faith—if they were together, he could face anything. The thali's flavours fell flat, so he ordered two bowls of fruit cream, remembering their old ice cream binges on Mumbai's streets. Kavya polished hers off and signalled the waiter for more, her sweet tooth a quirk that tugged a faint grin from him. He took one spoonful, the cream cloying against his tongue, his mind too tangled to taste it. Watching her, he wondered where he'd faltered. Why would she not fight for them as he did?

After dinner ended, they came outside to face the dark of the night. Rudra's grip on her loosened. Not physical, but emotional. She had to choose, even if it shattered him.

"Have you booked a place?" she asked, voice soft, searching his face.

"I'll figure it out soon," he said, casually.

They trudged to her hotel, steps dragging. He carried her bags, fingers lingering on the straps, and they slipped inside, his pulse quickening as the door clicked shut. He perched on the bed's edge, the mattress creaking under him, eyes tracing the room's faded wallpaper while she hovered nearby, her presence a pull he couldn't resist.

Her gaze met his, steady and deep, and then she crossed to him, settling onto his lap. She tilted her face up, tears glinting like dew, voice a fragile thread. "Rudra, I missed you."

"I missed you too," he rasped, eyes stinging, tears brimming.

"If we keep this up, how do we move on?" she asked, voice cracking.

"We'll find a way," he said, forcing strength into his words. "Trust me."

Empty promises, maybe, but he'd say anything to ease her doubt.

He'd come to Rajkot to rekindle something, to prove their love still burned, and now, holding her, he felt it. She loved him, fierce and true. That was enough to steel him against the odds, to fight for her place in his life. They stretched out on the bed, her head nesting on his arm, bodies curling into each other like roots seeking soil. They traded stories—of love, of life, of them—but doubt shadowed her words. "It'll be okay," he murmured, fingers threading through her hair, tracing her tear-streaked face. "Timing's off, but if we hold on, it'll work out." He needed her to believe, even if he wasn't sure himself.

Their eyes locked, and they kissed. Her tears tore at him. "No crying, Kavya," he whispered, brushing her cheek. "No sadness. Don't give up." He kissed the mole beneath her eye, a vow breathed against her skin. "We'll find our way back."

His heart unclenched at her smile. He felt like the world was righting itself.

"You're not uncomfortable, right?" he asked, voice low. "I can book somewhere else if you are."

"Stay with me," she pleaded, soft and sure.

He grinned, tugging her up. "Come on, there's a soda shop downstairs." A distraction, a stab at normalcy. As they walked, he spun a tale from Jamnagar. Election nights, guzzling soda with locals, a ritual he'd let slip in Mumbai's grind. "Gujaratis swear by it. Post-dinner, pre-sleep," he said, nostalgia warming his tone.

They ordered kala khatta sodas, the tart fizz snapping on their tongues, and shared a cigarette, smoke curling into the rain-damp night. When they finished, they drove through Rajkot's quiet streets, rain tapping the roof like a lullaby, closed shops blurring past. Time nudged them back to the hotel, steps light but hearts heavy, her bouquet and his bag in tow.

In the room, he swapped his shirt for a faded tee, brushing his teeth while she sprawled on the bed, too tired to join him. Her hair fanned across thc pillow. "What's with the flower count in that bouquet?" he asked, sliding beside her, voice playful, craving her spark.

They cuddled, bodies moulding together, an hour of quiet comfort before sleep claimed them. "I've barely slept this week," he murmured, voice fraying. "When'd you miss me most?"

"Every morning," she said, soft and raw. "Cried through our old talks."

Guilt stabbed him. He should've called. "Not calling you gutted me," he confessed. "Kept begging for a sign, then saw your exhibition post. I had to come. I can't lose you over someone else's bullshit take on me."

"My dad won't budge," she said, hopelessness seeping in.

He held her tighter, helpless but defiant, his love a fire that wouldn't die.

"Let's wait then," Rudra murmured, voice soft as a prayer, fingers brushing Kavya's arm. "Two, three months. Give it time before we push again." His heart strained for a fix, a way to stitch them back together.

She didn't answer. Words dried up between them, the quiet settling like dust after a storm.

Dawn crept in at 6:15 the next day. Rudra stirred, restless, his body humming with a need he couldn't name. He turned to Kavya, still lost in sleep, her face a serene sketch against the pillow. Lashes fanned over her cheeks, lips parted in a soft curve. His chest swelled, love flooding inside him like a tide. He slid closer, pressing a gentle kiss to her forehead, then her nose, tasting the warmth of her skin. He wanted to bottle her peace and nearness and etch it into his bones.

Her eyes fluttered open, sleepy and searching, finding his. Their lips met, slow and deep, a quiet exploration that sparked his pulse. "Kavya, I love you," he whispered, voice fraying at the edges.

She held his gaze, silent, something unspoken flickering in her eyes.

"Kavya, I love you," he said again, softer, pleading.

"Rudra, I don't want to string you along," she replied. "We… us… It can't work."

His heart plummeted, a cold, sharp drop. Their love, fierce as it burned, couldn't topple her family's walls. This felt final… a goodbye carved in whispers. "Kavya, was any of it real?" he asked, voice trembling, grasping at the past, desperate to believe it wasn't smoke.

"You're the best thing I've ever had," she said. "You made me so happy." She paused, breath hitching, emotions clawing free. "Rudra, I'm simple. Don't ever hurt me."

Her words sliced him, a blade twisted deep. "Kavya, it kills me you'd think that," he said, voice cracking with hurt. "I'd never harm anyone—least of all you." Her doubt stung, a bruise on his honesty, his openness with her now a wound.

"Sonakshi said you run with goons in Mumbai," she added, voice low, cutting sharper, echoing rumours that shadowed him.

"I know some, sure—in good faith," he shot back, frustration flaring. "I'm social, Kavya—always have been. My friends span every corner of life. People twist that, fine, but you? Thinking I'm some thug? That guts me. I've been real with you… never thought you'd judge me like them." His plea hung there, raw, begging her to see him clearly.

She didn't push back. And the topic died just like that, a ghost between them.

At 9:15, her alarm shrieked, shattering their fragile hush. It was a nudge that time was passing. He had to get to the exhibition; her day was a tightrope of tasks. They rolled out of bed, limbs heavy, hearts heavier, and she darted to freshen up.

Rudra watched, love tugging him toward her, eyes tracing her as she double-checked her things. "I never use hotel drawers," she muttered, methodical as ever. He grinned, proud of her quirks. He'd been sloppy, leaving his Nivea cream in the cupboard. She spotted it, tossing it his way with a playful flick. "Rudra, I told you to check, and you didn't," she chided, voice soft, eyes warm with a love he'd carry forever.

He threw up his hands, a mock surrender, grinning despite the ache. "Sorry," he apologised. She smiled, fingers grazing his jaw, and they hugged for a brief moment.

By 10:35, they bolted from the hotel, late and frantic, Kavya clutching the bouquet in a burst of whimsy. At the gallery, she paused. "Come in with me," she urged.

"Nah, I'll catch you tonight when you're done," he said, dodging the pull of her world.

"Okay, Rudra," she replied.

He gave her a slow, deliberate kiss. She vanished into the lift, and he turned away, hunger gnawing at him. He found his driver, and they hit a dhaba—aloo parathas and dal steaming on chipped plates, orange juice sharp on his tongue. The clock tower chimed noon as they finished.

"Drop me at a coffee shop," he told the driver, who shrugged. "Don't know this city, sahib."

Rudra scrolled his phone, spotting a Starbucks near the gallery. The driver left him there, and he stepped inside, the air cool with roasted beans. Ordering a cold coffee, he sank into a chair, the glass sweating in his hand, and let his mind churn.

He flagged a barista. "Got a notepad?"

Six sheets landed in front of him soon after. He stapled them.

His pen flew over the paper for the next two-and-a-half hours. Five pages of his life. His school days. The campaigns he had been on. The grind of politics he had to deal with.

He reread it, pride swelling, then scrawled at the end, "What I've done isn't for others to judge. Show this to your dad. Let him see me." Politics baffled most, especially her family, but he'd shaped a nation's pulse. He had no regrets there. He folded the note, tucking it into his shirt pocket, a first for him.

At 4:30, he drifted to a mall, eyeing a laptop in a gadget shop, killing time. At 5:30, he texted her.

RR: What time are you free?

KK: Rudra, an hour…ish… Come to the gallery.

RR: Be there by 6:30.

He hit a salon next—head massage, hair wash, forty minutes of oil and steam easing his skull. At 6:20, he stepped out, lit a cigarette, and slid into the cab.

Twenty minutes later, he marched upstairs to have Kavya's beautiful smile greet him. He dove in, hauling her suitcases. Two hulking ones bound for Nashik by courier.

"Aren't we late?" he asked, glancing at the clock.

"Flight's at 9:30," she said, calm as ever. "We need to be there by 8:30. It's 7:15—we'll leave in fifteen, hit the airport at 8:00. We're fine."

Her bag's zip fastener fought back, so he wrestled it shut, locking and taping the cases. By 7:40, they were set. She chatted with Anuradha, the gallery owner, who invited her to a February wedding. Hearing that, Rudra started dreaming about him and Kavya, spinning through garba, a future he hoped would come.

They rolled out at 7:45, rain slicking Rajkot's streets, traffic snarling the roads. Worry gnawed at him, but he filled the crawl with stories. The salon, the massage, his day. Her fingers slid through his hair. "Rudra, it's so soft!" she said, laughing.

He nodded, her hand finding his, holding tight the whole ride. "Our first trip together," she mused, voice light. "Can't believe you came all this way."

"Had to," he said, kissing her knuckles, her skin warm against his lips.

They hit the airport at 8:15. She pulled out her diary, pressing two sunflowers and two roses between its pages. "Can't take them all," she sighed.

"More'll come, bro," he said, grinning. "Flowers forever." She smiled back, and he hoisted her suitcase, slinging her bag over his shoulder. She grabbed his, a surprise that tugged at his heart.

Rudra trailed Kavya into the Ahmedabad airport, her silence a weight he carried as they snagged seats side by side at the counter, a stranger wedged between them. She glanced at the middle seat, shrugging. "I'll manage," she murmured, voice flat but steady. They checked in, only to hear the flight was delayed thirty minutes. Outside, they sank onto a weathered bench, her fingers lacing through his, gripping tight, her head dropping to his shoulder. She rubbed his knuckles, and the publicness of it—once a thorn—felt natural now, her touch sanding down his edges.

"Bro," he said, voice low, a grin tugging his lips, "never thought I'd be okay with this PDA stuff, but with you, it's good."

She smiled, soft and wordless, her eyes glinting under the terminal's harsh fluorescents.

"Hungry?" he asked, nudging her.

"Chocolate brownie sundae with extra nuts," she chirped, a spark flaring in her tone. He led her to the tuck shop, her arm hooked through his, clinging like ivy as the shopkeeper piled nuts atop the melting mess. Strangers' curious and judgmental stares skimmed over them, but Rudra let it slide, basking in her nearness. If anyone asked for his best moments, he'd point to this. Her hand on him, the sundae dripping, the world fading into the background.

Back on the bench, she leaned in, lips hovering near his. "Hold, bro, hold," he teased, stalling her kiss, heart thumping as if they'd rewound to before. Happiness surged, a wild, fleeting rush. "Rudra," she said, voice dipping, "I can't tell you how trapped I feel about marriage. The next guy I meet, I might just say yes."

He shook his head, firm but gentle. "No, Kavya, it's your call… your life. Take your time. We'll try again."

A flicker of hope licked at his chest. Maybe she believed in them still.

The flight announcement crackled, jolting them upright. They strode to the gate, her arm still tangled with his. She half-skipped beside him, joy bubbling up like soda fizz. Passengers grinned back, caught in their glow, and Rudra felt invincible, the walk a golden thread in his memory.

Onboard, the middle-seat guy wouldn't budge, but Kavya wouldn't settle. "We'll manage," Rudra said, but she prowled the aisle, hunting seats together. A grey-haired man swapped with a nod, and they claimed their spot, her kissing his cheek as they sank. She caught his flush, laughing. "Shy, huh?" He ducked his head, grinning.

The plane roared skyward.

He almost spilt about the Starbucks note, the pages burning a hole in his pocket, but held back, planning to slip it to her later. She sensed it, eyes narrowing. "What're you hiding?"

"Not telling," he said, smirking, and she squeezed him tighter. "Rudra, I'll lick your neck if you don't," she warned, voice playful, mischief dancing in her gaze.

"Bro, people are watching," he hissed, half-laughing, heat creeping up his neck.

"Don't care," she shot back, giggling. And he believed her.

The fun crashed when she murmured, "Two hours left, then I'm gone." Her words landed like a stone, sinking into his heart. He clammed up, sadness seeping in, and she quieted too, their hands still locked, emotions swirling thick as the clouds outside.

They landed in Mumbai, and she said, "Rudra, I'll book an Airbnb." He nodded but knew she'd stay with him, no question. He booked a cab soon after. As they walked, her hand slid into his back pocket, casual and bold. "What do you think of couples like this?" she asked, grinning.

"Judge 'em hard," he said, and they dove into old rants.

In the cab, she pressed, "You won't let me stay at an Airbnb, right?"

"Kavya, why ask when you know?" he countered, brow arched.

"It's not right," she insisted, voice soft but firm.

"Feels right to me," he said.

She gripped his hand as the cab sped off, her head lolling into sleep against his shoulder.

They rolled into his place at 1:00 A.M. She swapped her clothes for a loose tee and dove onto the bed, exhaustion claiming her. Rudra's stomach growled, so he ordered dal khichdi. It arrived in twenty-five minutes, steaming in a foil bowl. He perched beside her, peeling the lid, letting the earthy scent curl into the air. She stirred, nose twitching. "Rudra, gimme a bite," she mumbled, eyes half-open.

He slid the spoon to her lips. She propped up, chewing with a sleepy nod of approval. She stayed awake, snagging half the bowl, their quickest meal yet.

Then she flopped back, asleep in seconds.

He woke at 7:30, sunlight slanting through the blinds, and found her half-awake, eyes soft. He kissed her, gently and slowly. "I don't want to lose you like this," he said, voice rough with need.

Her eyes welled, glistening. "Rudra, I feel helpless," she whispered. "I don't know what to do."

"Keep faith in us," he urged, fierce and steady. "I'll handle the rest." She didn't reply, and doubt gnawed at him. He pressed on, spilling about work and his family, pulling the Starbucks notes from his pocket. "Read this… Show your dad. If he's got questions, he can call me." Sadness tugged. Why beg for her trust when she knew him? But she was here, wasn't she? That had to mean something.

She scanned the pages, voice soft. "Rudra, you've done so much."

"Yeah, bro," he said, grinning, "and I'll do more—get you that olive-green chartered plane you dream of." She lunged into a hug, arms tight. They cuddled, time blurring until she booked the Sitapur Express for 4:25 p.m., tucking their boarding passes into her collage. Hope flickered. Maybe she felt it too.

By 12:30, they scrambled to bathe. He had aloo parathas whipped up—two each, ghee-slicked and filling. A nap followed, and then at 2:45, he summoned a cab. They hit the station, the train was waiting, but the gates shut. So they perched on a stone slab, a pillar jutting through it like a spine. Wet eyes met wet eyes, hands clasped, neither wanting her to go.

"Kavya, we've gotta be our best selves for this," he said, voice thick.

"We will," she replied, nodding, a fragile promise.

"I won't call all the time, but let's talk sometimes," he said, and she agreed.

Fifteen minutes later, the gates creaked open, and they boarded, sinking into seats as a delay announcement hit. 6:40 p.m., not 4:25. Two extra hours gifted by fate. Others grumbled, spilling onto the platform, but Rudra and Kavya stayed put, hands locked, talking. She wished him luck, curiosity lighting her face.

Hunger struck, and he dashed out, returning with cold drinks, Little Hearts, Kurkure, and Masala Magic chips. They devoured it all, crumbs dusting their laps, time slipping to 6:30. A girl fumbled with her suitcase nearby, and Rudra's gaze lingered. For a tad bit longer than he wanted to.

Kavya's brows shot up, a smirk tugging her lips. "Unintentional, sorry," he muttered sheepishly.

She laughed, pinching his cheek. "I know, Rudra."

The train whistled.

Ten more minutes now. They shuffled to the gate, hugging fiercely and long, snapping three photos on their phones. They would be keepsakes. "Bro, no pressure," he said, voice steady. "Follow your heart. Meet who you need to, but give us a shot. We'll talk to your dad after Diwali—13th, 14th."

"Okay, Rudra," she said, eyes shining.

He kissed her mole, a final mark, and stepped off, heart as a stone, as the gates clanged shut. She stood there, hands pressed to the glass. He kissed her fingers through it, waving as the train pulled away, leaving behind a thin thread of hope.

Chapter 17

What Sonakshi Said!

THE mall's bright lights glared overhead, washing the corridors in a sterile glow, while garish displays of sequined clothes and trinkets flickered in Rudra's periphery. Shoppers jostled past, their chatter a dull roar, but he trudged through it all, eyes locked on the scuffed tiles beneath his boots, mind adrift. He'd thrown himself into work these past days. Anything to smother the ache gnawing at his chest. The protests might ease now, but Kavya's absence haunted him still, her face a ghost trailing every move, every call. He needed her—needed to see her, to fix this.

He'd grabbed a new phone, its box tucked under his arm, and was aiming for the exit when she appeared, standing by a jewellery stall, her profile sharp against the soft gleam of handcrafted bangles. Her expression stayed guarded, a mask he knew too well, and his heart lurched, a wild skip that stole his breath. Weeks had stretched since the station goodbye, and the urge to bridge that gap roared in his veins. He had to make her hear him, to peel back the lies clouding her view.

His steps slowed, deliberate, boots scuffing the floor as he closed in, heart hammering with a fragile hope. "Kavya," he said, voice low, barely cutting through the mall's hum.

She turned, eyes snapping to his—surprise flaring, then wariness dimming the spark. "Rudra," she replied, her tone strained, a whisper stretched thin over unseen fractures. Since the train pulled away, their thread had frayed, and he felt it now, a pang slicing deep.

He nodded, pulse thudding against his ribs, scrambling for words that wouldn't spook her. "How are you holding up?" he asked, keeping it light, his voice steady despite the storm brewing inside.

"I'm okay," she said, clipped and quick, her gaze sliding away—a wall rising, brick by subtle brick.

Rudra swallowed, treading carefully. He needed her to see, to dig into the rot Sonakshi had sown. "Been meaning to ask," he started, casual but pointed, "did Sonakshi ever give you anything solid on me? Like, what'd I do that was so unethical she had to judge me?"

Kavya's fingers drifted to a necklace, tracing its edge absently, her eyes clouding as if sifting through memories. She was weighing it, he could tell—each second a taut wire. Then she met his stare. "She showed Dad photos," she said, voice soft, hesitant, "you with some… associates. Said you're all about power and politics. She's worried for me. That's why she did it. I still think she means well."

His gut sank, a slow, cold drop. "So, no real dirt. Just pics and her spin?" he pressed, urging her to spot the flimsy thread Sonakshi dangled. "Nothing specific?"

She dipped her head, staring at the floor. "No," she murmured, barely audible, a confession that hung like damp smoke.

Frustration flared, hot and jagged, clawing up his throat. He wanted to shake her, to spill how those accusations had gouged him raw. "Kavya," he said, voice tightening, pain seeping through, "it cut me deep when you and your family questioned my ethics, my heart, who I am. Made me feel like you never knew me, like all we built, all I gave you, just… evaporated." The words tumbled out, a flood he couldn't dam, his hurt bared in the fluorescent glare.

Her eyes flicked up, wide with surprise, a glint of guilt shimmering there. Her lips parted—"I…"—but the sound faltered, snagging on something unspoken. She turned away. "I have to go," she said, her voice a faint echo, retreating fast.

He nodded, throat tight. She needed space—he got that—but their bond wasn't trash to toss. "Take care," he said, voice steady, though his chest ached as she slipped into the crowd, her figure blurring among the shoppers like a fading sketch.

His phone buzzed then, sharp and insistent. The manager's gruff voice barked through. "Rudra, get here. Meeting—now." Urgency crackled in the line, and he sucked in a breath, boots pivoting toward the exit. Work called a meeting to discuss the upcoming elections.

He stepped into the mall's parking lot, the air thick with exhaust and heat, and climbed into his cab. The city sprawled ahead, a jagged horizon, and he leaned forward, resolve hardening. He'd keep moving, keep battling.

For her. For them. Broken or not.

Even the familiarity of her home in Nashik felt oppressive to her as she remembered her meeting with Rudra at the mall. She had returned home from the mall, her heart conflicted by the ambiguous promises of help from political figures and her meeting with Rudra. She was tired, she was stressed, and she was longing for a moment of peace, a moment to collect herself and process her thoughts. She was exhausted from the events of the last few weeks. She just wanted a bit of calm.

She walked through the living room, her senses heightened, her mind still replaying the conversation with her artisans, the strange, almost surreal, offer of help from unknown political sources. There was a sudden urge to seek solace in the silence of her bedroom. She was about to enter her room when she heard the muffled sound of voices coming from her father's study, her footsteps halting instinctively. She recognised her father's voice, low and measured, but she also recognised the smooth, almost calculated tone of Sonakshi's voice, and her heart skipped a beat, a wave of suspicion washing over her.

She hesitated, her hand hovering over the doorknob, her mind racing, her curiosity warring with her desire to avoid another confrontation, another emotional battle. She had always been a calm, rational person, but Sonakshi's constant interference in her love life was getting to be too much. She decided to listen for a bit, her senses as sharp as ever, her instincts telling her that something was not right. She was tired of all the problems, tired of being stressed. She wanted to be free.

She pressed herself against the wall, her heart pounding against her ribs, her breath held captive in her chest, her ears straining to decipher the conversation.

"So, you said that you had some more information about Rudra." Her father's voice was soft but firm, the words a mixture of scepticism and a need to know everything. "What else is it that have you heard?"

Why was her father so interested in Rudra now that she had told him she could never be with him? And why was Sonakshi so obsessed with maligning Rudra's name in her father's ears even after she knew everything had been done and dusted between her and Rudra?

Sonakshi's voice, as always, was smooth and persuasive. "Uncle, you already know that Rudra is not who he seems. On top of that, I've been hearing things from people in Mumbai, from people who know him," she said. "He is very unethical, and he is all about using his position to gain personal profit. His actions speak of his character. He doesn't care about anyone else."

Kavya's heart sank, her fingers clenching around her phone. She knew that Sonakshi was using her charm to influence her father, that she was playing on his fears and his insecurities, and her carefully curated image of Rudra was slowly, and deliberately, being destroyed. She could feel her anger rising, her desire to stop this, to pull her away from her father's influence, growing stronger with each passing moment, and she was also finding it difficult to control her emotions.

"And they said that he might have a hand in the ongoing truck protests," Sonakshi continued, her voice now more dramatic. "They said that he is a man of violence, and he doesn't care about the community, and he's only trying to gain power by creating chaos. I felt like you should be aware, since you have been considering him for Kavya. I couldn't let her be with someone like him."

Kavya's blood ran cold. She had been so busy trying to manage her business that she had been ignoring the truth; her ability to see through Sonakshi's deceit had been clouded. She had no idea where Sonakshi was getting all this information from. She had no idea about her contacts.

Plus, she had no idea that her father was still considering Rudra. Didn't he strike him off the list? Wasn't he against Rudra in the first place?

"Thank you for sharing this with me, Sonakshi," her father said, his voice now filled with a mixture of scepticism and concern. "I appreciate your honesty. And now I am sure that he's not the right man for Kavya." He had made up his mind, and he wasn't going to change it now. He had always been very stubborn, and she had always known that about him.

Sonakshi let out a small laugh, a smug sound that sent a shiver down Kavya's spine. "Of course, Uncle," she said, her voice smooth and persuasive. "I only want what's best for Kavya, and I wouldn't want to see her get hurt by someone like that."

Kavya had heard enough; her patience finally reached its breaking point. She had always thought that Sonakshi was her best friend, that she would always support her, but now, she realised that she was wrong.

She pushed open the door and rushed inside. Both her father and Sonakshi looked at her, their faces betraying their surprise.

"What is going on here?" Kavya asked, her voice sharp, her eyes piercing. "Sonakshi, where are you getting this information about Rudra from? Why are you doing all of this?" She could no longer tolerate Sonakshi. She needed to know why she was acting like that, why she was so invested in her personal life. She wanted answers.

Sonakshi's face faltered, her smile faltering slightly, her composed demeanour finally cracking under the weight of Kavya's rage. "Kavya, it's not what you think," Sonakshi said, her voice a little more hesitant now.

"Then tell me, Sonakshi, where are you getting your information?" Kavya asked, her voice now cold, her eyes fixed on her best friend. "Who are these people that you have been in contact with?" She wanted to get to the bottom of this, and she was done with the lies.

"I was only trying to help," Sonakshi tried to convince her, her voice a mix of defensiveness and a desperate attempt to justify her actions. "I was only doing what was best for you."

Kavya looked at her, her eyes filled with a mixture of disappointment, disgust, and a deep sense of betrayal. "Stop helping me, Sonakshi," she said, her voice now a whisper, her tone reeking of finality.

Chapter 18

See You Later, Alligator

THE lawn sprawled wide under a canopy of fairy lights, alive with the clatter of wine glasses and bursts of laughter that rang like chimes in the warm night air. Kavya wove through the crowd, a ghost in the revelry, her smile a brittle veneer plastered over the churn in her gut. Faces blurred past—flushed cheeks, glinting eyes—but her own gaze darted restlessly, snagging on nothing, her mind tethered to Rudra. His voice from last week still echoed, raw and wounded, slicing through her like a shard of glass she couldn't shake.

She tried to anchor herself in the chatter, nodding at half-heard anecdotes, raising her glass to toast strangers, but her thoughts rebelled, dragging her back to him. His hurt was a mirror to hers, his words a relentless drumbeat of what she'd thrown away. Choices carved scars, she knew that now. Rudra's pain at the mall had been her doing, her silence a blade that severed him loose to move on. The ache for him flared, sharp and unbidden—his hands, his steady gaze—but she clenched her jaw, shoving it down. She had to stand firm, think straight, and bury the mess of her heart.

Sonakshi emerged near a table heaped with samosas and glistening kebabs, her laughter a high, theatrical trill cutting through the hum. She held court among a knot of acquaintances, gestures sweeping wide, her silk blouse catching the light like spilt ink. Kavya lingered back, watching, her stomach tightening. Sonakshi's poise was a performance. Every tilt of her head, every flash of her smile, was a polished act, her eyes glinting with a charm too sharp, too deliberate. This wasn't the Sonakshi she knew, the one who'd whispered warnings over chai. This was a stranger, a puppeteer tugging strings for an audience, and the dissonance prickled Kavya's skin.

Sonakshi's voice rose, steering the talk to herself, recounting some tale with exaggerated flair—hands fluttering, brows arching, a spotlight she'd crafted. Kavya's chest sank, unease curling like smoke. She'd never clocked it before. This hunger for attention, this calculated dance. Every laugh, every nod Sonakshi drew, felt rehearsed, a mask slipping to reveal something colder. Kavya's mind rewound. Sonakshi's sly nudges, her insistence on being right, the way she'd always bent Kavya's choices to her will. The barbs, veiled as care; the critiques, sharp as thorns; the quiet envy threading through years of friendship. Clarity crashed in, a tide ripping through fog. She'd been played, a marionette in Sonakshi's grip, blind to it until now.

Memories sharpened. Sonakshi's whispers about Rudra, seeding doubt like poison ivy. Those photos, grainy and skewed, spun into tales of power and goons. Her voice had dripped with concern, but it was a lie, a web to trap Kavya's trust. Sonakshi thrived on flaws, hers and others', her negativity a constant hum. Kavya had tuned out. Had she ever cheered Kavya's wins or just revelled in steering her course? The truth stung. Sonakshi's "care" was a sham; her moves fuelled by jealousy, a need to reign. Kavya's spine stiffened. She wouldn't swallow it anymore. She drew a breath, deep and steady, eyes locking on Sonakshi's glittering figure. The haze lifted. She saw the pattern, the game. Now, resolve hardened in her chest like iron cooling in a forge. No more bending, no more strings. She was Kavya, damn it, and she'd carve her own path, free of Sonakshi's leash. Her feet carried her forward, steps firm on the dew-slick grass, heart pounding but sure. She wouldn't let Sonakshi unravel her life, wouldn't let anyone dictate her soul. It was time to face her, to cut the ties, to claim what was hers—her choices, her love, her fight.

The lawn pulsed with life beneath the star-stitched sky. Laughter rippled through the crowd as silk sarees shimmered in the soft glow of string lights. Kavya felt her chest tighten, hardening her resolve to do what needed to be done. She spotted Sonakshi near the snack table, her crimson dupatta fluttering as she held court among admirers.

Kavya moved through the gathering with purpose, her lehenga brushing against her ankles. She gripped Sonakshi's arm firmly, cutting through whatever trivial conversation was underway.

"Come with me," she said, voice low but commanding. Something in her tone made Sonakshi follow without protest.

They reached a quiet corner near the jasmine hedge, the sweet scent hanging in the air as the party noise receded. Kavya turned to face her, struggling to control her breathing.

"You broke us, Sonakshi." The words emerged steadily despite the tremor in her hands. "Those photos, your lies… you deliberately sabotaged what Rudra and I had. I trusted you."

Sonakshi's lips parted, but Kavya continued before she could speak.

"No. I see everything clearly now. Your concern was calculated. You needed to control me, and when you couldn't, you destroyed what mattered most." She paused, feeling tears threaten but refusing to let them fall. "We're done. You're not my friend anymore."

Sonakshi's expression hardened, but Kavya didn't wait for a response. She turned away, heart pounding as she moved through the crowd, thinking only of Rudra.

Images flooded her mind. That first date when he arrived twenty minutes late, breathless with apologies and a single yellow marigold. The quiet evenings in his modest apartment, her head on his shoulder as they talked about nothing and everything. The afternoon they spent at the market, Rudra deliberated over purses for his sister's Rakshabandhan gift, his genuine care showing in the way he considered each option. The Rajkot exhibition, where he stood beside her, attentive to her excitement over each item she sold. The train station, his figure growing smaller as her train pulled away, his hand raised in farewell.

In each memory, she recognised the same truth: he had been steady, present, real. And she had let him go.

Kavya reached the lawn's edge and pulled her phone from her clutch. Her fingers trembled as she dialled his number. One ring. Two. Five. Nothing. She tried again, heart sinking as the call went unanswered.

She sat on a stone bench, her hands clutching her lehenga. The party continued behind her, indifferent to her pain. She looked up at the night sky, which cared not about her heartbreak.

Where had he gone?

She had wounded him deeply, letting doubt poison what they'd built together.

Kavya closed her eyes, her phone still clutched in her hand.

She'd lost him. Her Rudra, her anchor. Here she was, a Bollywood heroine adrift without her hero, chasing a love she'd let slip through her fingers.

The path forward lay muddled in front of her eyes, her mind churning with the different possibilities of her finding him in the chaos that was this city. As she sat thus, devoid of hope, a saying her teacher used to say at her boarding school came flashing in her mind.

Some journeys don't end with wound-up conclusions. Some stories continue beyond the final page, unresolved yet possessing a seed of hope. They simply wait for our courage to write the next chapter.

Acknowledgments

I would like to express my heartfelt gratitude to everyone who has been part of this journey of bringing the novel to life.

My deepest thanks go to **Varun Prabhu** and **Tanisha Aacharya** for their exceptional editing, thoughtful guidance, and constant encouragement. Their dedication and attention to detail have been invaluable in shaping the manuscript.

I am deeply grateful to **Lipika Bhushan** for her guidance and unwavering support, which played a crucial role in navigating this creative journey.

I am also grateful to **Prachi Sharma** for her careful proofreading; **Payal Barkeshia** for her creativity in design ideation and social media management; **Nikita Singh** for her consistent documentation; and **Sharad Singh** for his support in social media management.

To the readers, thank you for allowing these characters to live in your imagination. This novel is the result of many minds, many moments, and countless late-night reflections—and I remain humbled by the collaboration that made it possible.